THANK YOU!

Dawn Lister, Aaron Bearden, Jill Mueller, Tim Flanagan, Sheriff Mike Harrison, Dr, D.P. Lyle, Adam Ake (the Kinard not the California one), Michael Connelly, and the many, many friends, family, and Good Samaritans who helped us during the storm and its aftermath.

Thanks for all your invaluable contributions!

AND THE SEA BECAME BLOOD

A JOHN JORDAN MYSTERY THRILLER BOOK 21

MICHAEL LISTER

PULPWOOD PRESS

Ebook ISBN: 978-1-947606-35-7

Paperback ISBN-13: 978-1-947606-34-0

Hardcover ISBN: 978-1-947606-36-4

For Brad Price

I cherish our early adventures and appreciate your dedication, service, and friendship.

AND THE SEA BECAME BLOOD

Dear Diary,

I've decided to kill somebody.

I haven't decided who yet, but I've definitely decided to do it, and that's progress.

I've been going back and forth about it for a while—should I? Shouldn't I? And those thoughts have been mostly subconscious or at least not at the forefront of my shattered mind. But something changed today.

Today is the day. Mark it down. Today is the day I decided to try my hand at death.

Because I could not stop for Death,

He kindly stopped for me;

The carriage held but just ourselves

And Immortality.

I am that carriage, a horse-drawn hearse —delivering death to some unsuspecting bastard.

I'm not completely sure why I'm doing it, not even when I'm lucid like now. I just know I want to. I want to try it. Try something new and different. Why not?

I don't think it will be particularly fun or especially exciting exactly, but it could be very instructive.

Is there a God? Or if not, is there any moral order to the universe? Will any force attempt to intervene to stop me?

Here's a hint, Diary, God or the universe or whatever SOB is in charge didn't ever stop any bad shit from happening to me, so . . . I think I already have my answer, but I'll know for sure soon. Very soon.

I suspect that the inmates are running the asylum. And this inmate right here is about to take another inmate off the board.

Now to figure out who.

Who shall I kill?

The perfect murder needs the perfect victim.

Shouldn't be too hard to find.

1

I am standing at the water's edge at sunrise, gazing out over the horizon.

In the east, the last streaks of pale bubblegum pink are giving way to a bright ripe tangerine orange as dawn turns to day.

The early October morning is still and serene and nearly silent, the cool currents of its briny air fresh as the newness of the day itself.

Below the glass bowl sky, the undulating surface of the green Gulf is hazy and hypnotic, its ancient rhythms as mysterious as the moon still visible overhead.

Beneath the beauty and serenity of sky and sea and the peace and comfort they evoke within me, a slight sense of dreadful foreboding scratches at the edges of my subconscious, like an idle finger worrying the fraying fringe of a favorite garment.

Without walking up, Dave Lloyd appears next to me.

Without speaking, he says, *Hark, now hear the sailor's cry.*

I nod as I look back out at the vanishing point where sea and sky become one, and let myself float into the mystic.

As if muted by distance, like music heard from a back-yard party a neighborhood away, Dave's acoustic performance of the haunting Van Morrison classic echoes through the empty halls of the abandoned mansion inside me.

I think about how unexpectedly and shockingly early the foghorn had called Dave home, and I wonder how long it will be before I hear it.

I don't fear that inevitable foghorn, but I'm not ready to set sail from this shore just yet.

Thought leads to thought like way leads to way, and the foghorn becomes a clanging buoy bell.

No man is an island, entire of itself. Every man is a piece of the continent, a part of the main.

Never send to know for whom the bell tolls.

Suddenly I am forlorn, my previous peace flung far from me like a bird in a storm.

Forlorn! the very word is like a bell to toll me back from thee to my sole self!

There are so many things I want to say to Dave, so many questions I have for him, but I am unable.

I miss our talks, the comfort of his compassion, the gentle challenge of his warm wisdom, the amusing, penetrative insight of his wit.

I want to tell him how I'm doing, need to share with him the counterintuitive sense of dread as I gaze at the calm beauty and majesty of the morning before me.

I'm about to turn toward Dave, to attempt to communicate with him in some way, but as I begin to, something on the horizon catches my eye.

It's so far away, so small from this distance, all I can make out is a flicker, some sort of shimmering disturbance like heatwaves around a mirage.

Wondering what it is, I turn toward Dave just in time to see him dissolving into the day, ever tinier particles, being drained of solidity, disappearing completely.

When I turn back toward the horizon, it is undergoing the same process.

Glancing down at my hands I see that I am too.

2

I wake on Monday morning just a little over 48 hours before Hurricane Michael hits to find myself alone in bed, my phone vibrating on the table next to my badge.

Still disturbed by witnessing the world dissolve around me, I'm disoriented, confused at first that Anna is not in bed with me.

Had she shattered into a billion particles too?

Then I remember she's in court this morning, and a little of my disconcertion dissipates.

Maybe she's who's calling.

Reaching for my phone, I recall that Carla is keeping Taylor and that I have a meeting about the storm at the prison just before lunch.

Anna, insisting I sleep in a little, had taken Taylor to

Carla's, our sometime sitter, and I suspect turned off my alarm.

Squinting at the face on my phone at the end of my extended arm, I see that it is Reggie, the Gulf County sheriff and my boss.

"Good morning, sunshine," she says.

"Morning," I say, and it comes out not unlike a low guttural growl.

"It's a bitch, I know," she says, "but suspicious death doesn't honor days off."

"Which is why you're smart enough to have three investigators in your department," I say.

"It's true, I *am* smart, but Darlene is on vacation and Arnie is in court this morning—probably gettin' his ass handed to him by your wife."

I kick off the covers. Early October in Florida is still summer and even with the central air on, a box fan, and a window unit running, I'm sweating a little.

"But even if Darlene and Arnie were around," she says, "you'd want this one anyway. We got a 911 call saying Father Andrew is dead inside his . . . home or church or whatever it is."

Andrew Irwin is a retired Catholic priest who I worked with at both Potter and Gulf Correctional Institutions. A gangly, emaciated, elderly man with wispy white hair, blue-blue eyes, bushy eyebrows, and the general unkempt appearance of an unmade bed, Father Andrew is a bit awkward and odd, but wise and kind too. Rarely not seen in the company of his beloved mastiff, Mary, Andrew's black suits and clerical shirts were perpetually covered in the fine buckskin hairs of the enormous dog—often accompanied by some of her drool.

"You haven't confirmed anything yet?" I ask.

"Wanted you to be the first one in," she says. "Figured you'd want to be . . . and seeing's how you live less than a mile away . . . figured you could be there about as fast as anybody."

"Who reported it?"

"Wouldn't leave his name. We're trying to get a trace on the phone used now. Whole thing could be a hoax or the guy who called could've killed him. Just don't know."

"Did the caller say something suspicious?" I ask. "Why would you jump to the possibility that—"

"Yeah, he did," she says. "I'll get a copy of it for you, but not being willing to leave his name is pretty suspicious in itself."

"Okay, I'll head over and check it out in a few," I say. "I sure hope it's a prank and he's not actually dead."

"Let me know what you find and what you need."

Still disquieted by the dream, I shower quickly and get dressed, my sense of unease heightened by my isolation. I rarely ever wake up in an empty bed, let alone a vacant house.

As I'm getting ready, I listen to the radio to get a storm

coverage update. As of this morning Michael is still a tropical storm, its 70-mile-per-hour winds sitting just under hurricane strength. The female meteorologist on the CBS station I'm listening to predicts that Michael will become a hurricane later today and reach landfall as a Category 2 by midday on Wednesday. She is unable to say exactly where the storm will hit but has the entire Florida Panhandle in a cone of uncertainty.

The storm coverage only intensifies my sense of dread and foreboding.

I can still see Dave dissolving. Can still feel myself flying apart, my essence a million tiny pieces flung far by the morning breeze.

I'm putting on my gun and badge when my phone vibrates.

I lift it from the bedside table to see that it's a text from Carla. *He's here again.*

On my way, I text back, and rush out.

3

When I pull onto Main Street, I head in the opposite direction of the crime scene.

Carla's text means the crime scene, if that's what it is, will have to wait.

He's here again means that Rudy, Carla's addict dad, has shown up unannounced at her apartment again where she is keeping her son, John Paul, and my and Anna's daughter, Taylor—something he's been doing with increasingly regularity.

Rudy raised Carla on his own—if you can call it that. She pretty much raised herself. He was an absentee father and an absentee diner owner. Carla had run the diner and parented herself and her dad. Shortly after becoming a mother, Carla moved out—leaving Rudy alone for the first time in his life. He has since closed the diner and spends his time on the road between Pottersville and Mexico Beach where his brother lives, often stopping by Carla's place, which is about the halfway point.

More a nuisance drunk than a mean one, Rudy's unscheduled appearances are more disruptive than anything else, but even without meaning to be, an inebriated person is a potentially dangerous person—especially one as old and awkward and thoroughly pickled as Rudy.

When I turn in to Moss Creek Apartments, I see Rudy's giant old red Cadillac parked at an odd angle nowhere close to a parking spot.

Finding an open spot near the antique automobile, I park and get out.

Moss Creek is a small government-assisted apartment complex on the south edge of town. As a single mom with a very low income, Carla qualifies, but it is thanks to Anna's tireless efforts on her behalf that she was able to secure one of the coveted units here.

Moss Creek has many rules—especially about visitors. If Rudy continues showing up here drunk and causing a disturbance or passing out in the parking lot, he's going to get Carla kicked out.

I find Rudy sprawled out on the front porch of Carla's apartment, snoring loudly.

Stepping over him, I tap on the door and walk inside when Carla opens it.

"*Daddy*," Taylor squeals, and runs over to me.

My core is reduced to uncooked cookie dough.

She hasn't been calling me *daddy* for long—only starting it recently after her own father died—and though it still catches me by surprise, I'm absolutely adoring the process of growing accustomed to it.

"Morning, angel," I say, picking her up and pulling her into an intense hug. "How are you?"

Looking like a little Anna, Taylor has huge brown eyes, smooth olive-tinted skin, and thickening light brown hair. She looks remarkably like my daughter, Johanna—something that shouldn't be surprising given that everyone has always said how much Anna and I look alike. The four of us look like what we are—a family.

"*Ga-ra-ate*," she says. "Carla's about to color with me. Do you want me to color you a picture, Daddy?"

"More than anything," I say. "Will you?"

"'Course, silly."

"Thank you."

I turn my attention to Carla, who is holding John Paul on her hip, bouncing him about a bit as she does.

She looks as she always does these days—perpetually tired, wired, haggard. Her shortish blond hair appears unbrushed, her pale skin appears bloodless, and the dark, half-moon circles beneath her eyes have that hint-of-plum coloration like bruises.

"You okay?" I ask.

She nods. "When I wouldn't let him in he threw a fit —yellin' and cussin', but eventually he just laid down and passed out."

"I was going to try to talk to him, but I'll let him sober up first," I say. "I'll have a deputy pick him up and take him down to the—"

"Please don't have him arrested," she says. "Please. Can't you just deal with it ... unofficially?"

Instantly I feel irritable.

I had hoped she had made a clean break from her dad, that she was going to do right by her little boy, and I have very little patience for her continuing to coddle him. Intellectually I know there are no clean breaks, of course, but emotionally I'm extremely frustrated that she's not finished with him and never will be.

"I've got a crime scene to be at," I say, and I can hear the anger in my voice. "Besides, if you don't start setting some boundaries and letting him suffer some consequences—"

"I know, but ..."

"Carla, I know it's hard, but ... you have your own son now. He should be your first priority. If this doesn't stop you could lose everything. Wind up homeless. And I can't let Taylor or Johanna keep coming over if there's always a good chance that Rudy's going to show up in an altered state."

When I think of the type of turbulent childhood she's condemning John Paul to it rends my heart.

"I know. I do. But . . . I feel so sorry for him. He's harmless. Just . . . well . . . he's pathetic."

"If you don't do this it's only going to get worse."

Given the fact that Carla's mom took off when she was a small child and that her dad is the only parent she's ever had, and given the fact that she has been far more a parent to him than he has her in the past decade, and given the dynamics of addiction in their relationship, I know what I'm asking her is probably something she's not capable of doing. But I've got to keep asking it of her because it's the greatest hope for her and her son.

"Setting boundaries and saying no to my alcoholic mom was one of the most challenging things I ever did," I say. "I know what I'm asking you to do. And I'm asking it of you because I know how critical it is that you do it—for John Paul's future."

The future little John Paul almost had was a very different one. Originally, Carla had asked me and Anna to adopt him, which we were all set to do until she changed her mind shortly after having him and holding him for the first time. And as difficult as it has been, I'm glad John Paul will be raised by his own mother. But I do find it infuriating when I feel as if she is putting him at risk.

She nods. "I know. I do. But . . . I'm sorry. I just can't. I can't turn him away. I can't turn him in. I'm sorry I just can't."

"You wouldn't just be doing it for you and your son," I say, "you'd be doing it for him too. If he never experiences any consequences . . . he'll never make any changes."

"I'm sorry," she says, shaking her head. "I really am."

Her lower lip is quivering, her head slightly bowed, and her eyes are downcast.

"I know," I say. "It's okay. What I'm asking you is . . . Don't be down on yourself for not being able to do it yet."

"I'm so weak and pathetic," she says. "No surprise there though. I come by it naturally."

That hurts my heart and fills me with enormous pity for her. I remind myself that she's doing the best she can, that I'm expecting too much too quickly and that my impatient insistence on certain ideals is only inflicting additional damage to her already bruised and beaten and nearly non-existent self-esteem.

"You're nothing like weak or pathetic," I say. "Nothing. I'm sorry. I didn't mean to . . . You're brave and strong and you're doing so well—building such a great life for you and John Paul."

"But—"

"Everything's going to be okay," I say. "It will work out. We'll figure it out."

She gives me a nod but I can tell she doesn't believe my lies any more than I do.

I feel defeated and deflated.

"You okay, *Daddy*?" Taylor asks.

"I sure am, big girl," I say, trying to rally out of the funk induced by my dream and the feeling of futility brought on by dealing with Carla and Rudy. "I'm just sad I have to leave you and go to yucky ol' work. But give me a super big hug and I think I'll be able to manage."

She does.

"*Wow*," I say. "One of the best hugs *ever*. That was epic. Thank you."

"Anytime, *señor*," she says, using the phrase her older sister taught her.

And just like that all my heaviness is gone, and I find myself with a wide grin on my face.

4

———

fter calling in unofficial backup to deal with
Rudy, I'm driving to the other end of Main
Street to the old Catholic church.

I had made three calls in pursuit of assistance with
Rudy. Finding Merrill unavailable I moved on to Dad.
Finding Dad unavailable I moved on to my brother, Jake.
So with Jake on Rudy duty, I drive along the morning
sun-dappled blacktop of Main beneath ancient oaks and
pines in October heat that feels like August.

Since moving to Wewahitchka from Pottersville, I
have fallen in love with the place, and it has become
home to me and my family in ways I didn't think possible.
A tiny town of extraordinary natural beauty, Wewa also
has some of the very best neighbors in the world.

Of the many decent and kind residents of our new

home, Father Andrew Irwin is one of the most beloved—at least from a distance. If he's really dead I have a hard time believing someone killed him.

The former St. Lawrence Catholic Mission is located at the far north end of Main Street, just beyond the new Ace Hardware and Ake's Septic Service. Beyond it there are only woods and a random smattering of houses.

Pulling into the long, wide driveway, I look around for any signs of disturbance or death but see none.

The building of St. Lawrence looks like what it has become—a house. The beige brick structure is wide and narrow, roughly the shape of airplane wings. All of the signage is gone, and the only hints that the dwelling hasn't always been a house are a large cross on the south side and the wide cement driveway with plenty of parking.

Religion this deep into the Deep South is mostly of the Baptist and Pentecostal variety, everything gradations of Protestant Fundamentalism, and as I understand it this small Catholic mission was only constructed here by the diocese when the state placed a prison here. Evidently the diocese believed that at least some of the families that travel to visit their incarcerated loved ones would be Catholic and want to attend Mass while in town. But most of the impoverished families of state inmates, Catholic or otherwise, don't travel our long state for the chance to see their dad, brother, or son for a few hours a few days a month. They can't. After years of only some variation of just six partial families attending, the diocese had abandoned St. Lawrence like the many Spanish missions that once lined the landscape when La Florida was part of the Captaincy General of Cuba.

At one time Father Andrew Irwin served as parish priest for a few different churches in the area—covering smaller congregations not large enough for their own full-time priest. Eventually when Andrew retired and inherited a large sum of money from his family, he purchased the shuddered former church and made it a home so he could settle down and live out his remaining years in this little town he came to adore.

Parking some twenty feet away from the building, I pull out my phone and begin recording.

Getting out of the car, I walk around the perimeter of the beige brick house, careful where I'm stepping and what I'm doing as I examine the yard and the building.

Morning dew still clings to everything—the grass beneath my feet, the green leaves of Andrew's garden, Ake's red dump trucks and white tanker trucks lining the south side of the property.

All doors and windows are closed. Nothing seems disturbed or out of place.

Behind his home, Andrew's garden, which looks to have corn, cucumber, and cauliflower, is thick and bountiful.

Before knocking on the door or entering the dwelling, I make sure to look in every window and door to see what might be seen from the outside. There is no sign of Father Andrew. If he is dead inside, whoever placed the 911 call would have to have been inside with him and not just seen him from out here.

I knock on the front door, identify myself, and yell for Andrew.

And get no response.

I repeat the process a few times at each door.

I realize that I still have Andrew's number in my phone from when he volunteered for me at the prison, so I withdraw my phone and call him, hoping that he still has the same number.

I can hear his phone ringing inside the building.

I wait.

It is accompanied by no other sounds—no movement, no radio or TV, no one talking, and no one answering the phone.

Based on the 911 call, the lack of response from my knocking, and the fact that I can hear his phone ringing inside, I decide I have probable cause to enter, and I begin trying the door knobs.

The front and side doors are locked but I find the back door unlocked.

Snapping on latex gloves and continuing to record

everything, I open the back door and yell for Andrew, identifying myself and my reason for being here.

And still get no response.

It's dim inside and it takes a few moments for my eyes to adjust.

The building smells of must and mothballs and dog but I can detect no hint of death or decay.

I feel around and locate a light switch and when I flip it on I see that I'm in a small, simple kitchen. The impersonal kitchen is all about function and nothing about form and is left over from when this was a church.

On the far wall are Mary's food and water bowls—both partially full. Above them on the wall is a mastiff calendar with her vet visits, grooming appointments, and medicine schedules handwritten in pen in the various boxes. I can tell the unopened bag of dog food in the corner is gourmet and expensive. Andrew won't spend money on himself but only buys the best for Mary. A quick glance shows the love and concern he lavishes on her, and how regimented and precisely scheduled is her care—checkups every quarter, grooming the first of every month, and on and on.

When I click on the light in the next room I can see that it is Andrew's living area—a small, modest couch and a well-worn chair sit empty apart from a frayed lap blanket in front of a dusty 40-inch TV on a stand. Traces of Mary's hair and drool are on everything. A few family photographs in mismatched frames hanging on the wall and a random bookcase with mostly old theology textbooks make the room more sad than homey—and the bedroom beyond is no different. More a monk's cell than a modern American bedroom, it is obvious Andrew is leading a very Spartan existence—something he's likely done his entire adult life.

I had often wondered why Andrew left the priesthood but now see that he hasn't—at least in terms of lifestyle.

There are two indentations in the covers on the bed. One appears to be Andrew's, the other is obviously Mary's, and as on the other furniture in the house her hair and drool are also present—only more so.

From his small, sparsely furnished living area I step out into what used to be the main sanctuary and search for the light switch.

When the lights finally flicker on I am surprised to discover that this part of the building is still set up like a sanctuary—with an aisle and rows of pews and an altar and lectern up front.

In fact, it looks just the same as it did when I was last here for a funeral a few years back.

It's as if Andrew's house has a church in it.

At a quick glance the only thing I see missing from the sanctuary is the large wooden crucifix that hung on the back wall behind the altar.

I call out for Andrew again and continue farther into the sanctuary searching for him.

The carpet and pews of the once consecrated space show traces of Mary, her hair, her drool.

I haven't taken very many steps down the center aisle when I see him.

Lying in a near fetal position on the floor between the first pew and the altar, the three-foot crucifix from the back wall cradled to him, Andrew, in only his underwear, is unmoving and unresponsive.

I rush over to him and, though it's obvious he's dead, check for a pulse.

He's stiff and his skin is cold and his body is inhumanly still.

He's dead. And has been for a while.

It's disconcerting to see Andrew in only his underwear—and not just because of the vulnerability and lack of dignity involved in having his pale, wrinkled old body displayed this way, but because until this moment I had never seen him in anything except a black suit and Roman collar. Even after he retired he still wore the black suit and clerical shirt—just without the small white tab.

Seeing Mary's dried slobber on his face and hairs on his body reminded me again of how close they were and how much joy she brought him.

Stepping back and getting both videos and pictures of

the body, I quickly scan the area, searching for any signs of foul play, ensuring no one else is here.

Within moments I determine that there are no obvious signs of a disturbance and I am the only living soul in the sanctuary.

I call for Mary but get no response.

An elderly man, nude except for his underwear, cuddling a large wooden crucifix, is a disturbing tableau, and I have to remind myself that the optics alone do not constitute a suspicious death.

I carefully step back over to the body, turning on the flashlight on my phone and examining it much more closely.

There are no signs of violence, no evidence that Andrew did anything but remove the large crucifix from the wall, lie down with it, and go to sleep.

And yet.

There's something odd about the entire scene and the way the body lies in situ.

Andrew is clinging to the cross like a drowning man to a piece of driftwood, and I find the image disquieting —and would even if he were fully dressed.

I'm about to call the crime scene unit and the medical examiner's office when something catches my eye.

There protruding the tiniest of fractions from his infinitesimally parted lips is what appears to be a bright blue speck.

It's so small at first I think it's a tiny spot of a liquid substance but given the color I can't imagine what it could be.

But then leaning down for a closer look I can see that it's a small piece of flat blue plastic.

After taking several pictures of it, I reach down and slowly and carefully pull it from Andrew's mouth.

What comes out is a small Roman cross someone has cut out of thin, bright blue plastic.

The material is extremely light—strong but flexible.

After studying it for a moment I think I might know what it's from—but then I get a whiff of it, and the sweet smell of pancakes and maple syrup let me know for sure.

Dear Diary,

I did it. I am death! Or last least his carriage. I picked out a person—more about that in a minute—and I did a little internet research (easy peasy) and presto deatho ding dong the old dude is dead.

Grass of levity,

Span in brevity,

Flowers' felicity,

Fire of misery,

Winds' stability,

Is mortality.

God, it was so much easier than I ever thought it would be. You would think taking someone's life, that thing that is most precious to them in all the world would be hard, but it's really kind of easy. It should require more. It should not only take more of an effort, but it should also be more monumental. In truth, it was kind of anti-climactic. Don't get me wrong, I'm glad I did it, but it wasn't even much of a rush. Of course, that's not why I did it, so it doesn't matter. I did it to see if I could—to see if God would stop me, to see if there is a God. I did it to see how it would feel—and the truth is I didn't feel much of anything.

As far as who I offed. It was just this sad old man. Can't imagine anyone will miss him much—except one old lady that seems to pine after him. It was almost like picking his name out of a hat. Was pretty random. I wanted someone who had no real connection to me, but whose house I access to.

I don't think anybody will suspect me, but even if they did, that's all it would be—suspicion. They could never prove anything. But I don't think anyone will even do that.

I may have committed the perfect murder.

For some reason, Raskolnikov keeps coming to mind, though I'm not sure why. I know my mind doesn't work right and I keep forgetting to remember things, so I've probably just forgotten why, but I'll tell you who I really think I should be compared to is Leopold and Loeb. Don't you?

What do you mean you don't know who they are? Dumb Diary!

Nathan Leopold and Richard Loeb, the rich students attending the University of Chicago who decided to commit the perfect crime to demonstrate their mental superiority— though that's not why I'm doing it. Or at least not the only reason. Mine is more to ask a question of the universe. Do you give a fuck? Does anything matter? Wait, that's two questions, but you get the point. Anyway, ol' Leopold and Loeb kidnapped and killed a kid named Bobby Franks. They fucked up and got caught, and who knows I might too, but it's not looking like it. Not at all.

Why am I thinking of Alfred Hitchcock? I'm not sure. My mind is fuckin' with me again.

Anyway—oh, yeah. I remember. Ol' Hitchcock made a movie based on Leopold and Loeb. What was the name of it? Why can't I remember anything these days?

A quick Google search and . . . The movie is called Rope on account of the boys who represent Leopold and Loeb in the film use a rope to off some poor sap named David. At least I think that was his name. Maybe that was the name of the—It doesn't matter. Nothing does, does it? Isn't that what my little experiment has proven?

"I haven't worked here long," she says. "You probably need to talk to the owners or their kids, but they're all on a cruise right now."

While the crime scene unit is processing the house and the medical examiner's office is processing the body, I've decided to start canvasing Andrew's neighbors.

My first stop is Ake's Septic Service, a family owned and operated business located in an old body shop building to the south of St. Lawrence's.

I find Ake's empty except for McKenzie Kemp, a temp worker hired to answer the phones while the Akes are away.

A recent graduate from Wewa high, McKenzie doesn't seem nearly as concerned about college or a career as she does about her phone. She's texting and checking her social media feeds while we talk—well, while I attempt to talk to her.

"They cruise during hurricane season?" I ask.

"They cruise *all* the time," she says distractedly without looking up from her phone.

"Can't imagine they could've built up this successful business if they really cruised *all* the time," I say.

"Huh?" she says, her head still down, her thumb busy scrolling through her Instagram feed. "Oh, well, I just meant they like to cruise. I come in and answer the phones while they're gone. They'll be back tomorrow."

The top of McKenzie's head, which is mostly what I'm seeing of her, is covered by thin blond hair with dark roots that falls in soft curls to the nape of her neck. Her bangs are swept back and held into place by gold bobby-pins.

"Thanks. I'll come back then and talk to them. But let me ask you a few questions while I'm here. Do you mind putting down your phone for a minute?"

It takes a moment for my words to register, but when they do, she looks up at me slowly and dramatically, her hazel eyes narrowed in confusion and disdain.

She discards the phone by tossing it carelessly on the desk and it thuds loudly, and I wonder how she can treat something that means so much to her so roughly.

"Thank you," I say. "This won't take but a minute. Did

you ever see Father Andrew or have any interaction with him?"

"Some . . ." she says. "I guess. Mostly saw him walkin' his dog or workin' in his garden. He was always nice. Sweet, you know?"

"When's the last time you saw him?"

She shrugs. "Yesterday maybe. Not sure exactly. But I think it was— Yeah, it was yesterday. Oh, wow, now that I think about it . . . he was . . . I don't know he seemed sort of unsteady on his feet. I didn't think anything of it. Well, I guess I thought it was just old age or the a-a-a-a-a-alcohol. Dang, I feel bad now. I guess I should've checked on him or something. But I really didn't think anything of it, you know?"

"Do you remember what time it was?" I ask.

Her entire face furrows in the exaggerated effort of recall. "It was before the mail came . . . so 'round ten, probably."

"And you thought he might be drunk?"

She shrugs. "Guess it crossed my mind. Sort of idly like. You know when you're kind of distracted like. Doing something else I guess. Wouldn't have thought of it again if you hadn't asked me about it."

"Did you often see him stumbling around or seeming drunk that early in the morning?"

She shakes her head slowly. "No."

"Ever?"

"No. Never, I guess. Only yesterday."

I nod. "He wasn't drunk. He didn't drink."

"Then what was it?" she asks.

"Have you seen anyone over there in the last few days?"

She shakes her head again, adding a frown to it this time. "Can't remember ever seeing any visitors. *Ever.* Guess he led a lonely old life. 'Course I'm not here much."

Unable to restrain herself another moment, she snatches up her phone and starts scrolling through it again.

"Even when you are, I guess," I say with a smile.

"Huh?" she says without looking up.

6

From Ake's I walk over to Ace Hardware.

A relatively new business in town, Ace is located in what had once been an independent hardware and then later a truss plant.

It's a large, clean, well-stocked store—especially for the size of the town.

I find Dawn Lister, one of the managers, in her office.

A forty-something woman in jeans and a red Ace sport shirt, she has striking greenish eyes, a dark complexion, and dishwater blond hair pulled back in a ponytail.

The wood-paneled walls of her office are mostly empty and her desk has the not too chaotic cluttered look of a truly productive person.

"What can you tell me about Andrew Irwin?" I ask.

"Who?" she says. "Oh, Father Andrew? Why? Is he okay?"

"Does he ever come over here? Do y'all ever have any dealings with him?"

She nods. "Sure. He passes by every day walking his dog. Stops and talks if we're out front. Comes in and buys dog food from time to time. Other odds and ends. Brings us vegetables from his garden. He okay?"

I shake my head.

Her narrow eyebrows shoot up. "He dead?"

I nod.

"What happened?" she asks.

"That's what I'm trying to find out. When's the last time you saw him?"

"Yesterday," she says. "I was out front getting the mail when he passed by. He didn't look so good. Kind of pale and unsteady. I asked if he was okay. He said he was dizzy and felt like he might pass out. I helped him over to a chair on our front porch and got him a bottle of water. He was unsteady on his feet, kind of uncoordinated in all his movements, and he was slurring his speech somewhat. I thought he might've been drinking but I didn't smell any on him. I asked if he wanted me to call an ambulance or take him to see Dr. Barnes, but he said he didn't, that he was okay. He sat for a while and seemed to get better. One of the girls who works here got some water for his dog. They just hung out here for a while. When he got to feeling better I had one of the guys who works here walk him home and make sure he got inside okay. I meant to check on him later in the day but I got slammed. I did send Levi, that's the guy who walked him home, back over to make sure he was okay later that afternoon."

"And was he?"

"Well . . . I assumed he was when Levi didn't tell me any differently, but I was with a customer when he came back."

"Can you call him in so we can talk to him?" I ask.

"He's out on a delivery right now. He'll be back this afternoon."

"Could you give me a call when he gets back?" I ask, handing her my card.

"Sure. No problem."

"Thanks."

I stand.

"You're an investigator," she says. "That mean there's something suspicious about the way he died?"

7
———

"You were right," Jessica says. "At least they think you are. They'll know for sure once the lab has had a chance to look at it."

Jessica Young is the Gulf County Sheriff's Department non-sworn crime scene tech. She is a plain-looking, midtwenties woman with a petite build and straight blond hair pulled back in a ponytail. She is smart and earnest and invested in her job. And because she is quiet or private or both, I don't know more about her than that.

While I have been canvasing she has been working with the FDLE crime scene crew and an investigator from the medical examiner's office to process the scene and the body.

We are standing at the back of the sanctuary watching

as the body is removed and the techs finish gathering the last of the evidence.

During the investigation it will be Jessica who coordinates with the lab and manages the forensic evidence.

"Witnesses statements seem to confirm it too," I say.

She nods.

Based on the sweet smell of the substance on the blue plastic cross placed in Andrew's mouth, I thought it likely he died of ethylene glycol poisoning, and though the autopsy and lab tests will have to confirm it, she's saying the techs and the ME investigator tend to agree.

Before either of us can say anything else, a short, balding crime scene tech walks over to us. He's still suited up and the too-big-for-him jumper makes his movements look awkward and comical.

He removes his mask to reveal a large, thick handlebar mustache underneath.

The long, elaborate facial hair is unexpected and looks absurd on this little man in the oversized bunny suit.

"So, we'll have to wait for lab results to be sure, but I'm inclined to agree with you. I think the substance on the object in the mouth, which you should not have removed, by the way, is most likely antifreeze. It doesn't necessarily follow that he died of ethylene glycol poisoning but gun to my head I'd say he did."

I nod. "Witnesses I've spoken to so far described symptoms consistent with it."

Reggie arrives and walks over to join us.

"Whatta we got?" she asks.

"Looks like ethylene glycol poisoning," the little FDLE tech says.

"What?" she asks.

"Antifreeze."

"He drank antifreeze?" she says.

"It's odorless and tastes sweet," he says. "Doesn't take much to be fatal. It'd go unnoticed in most drinks—orange juice, Kool-Aid, coffee, energy drinks. Depending on how much he drank it could take up to a couple of days—during which time he'd experience symptoms of intoxication, abdominal pain, vomiting, headaches, eventually loss of consciousness, seizures. All the while brain damage and kidney failure is happening."

She looks at me. "We thinking he did it to himself?" she asks.

I shake my head.

"If you're using it to commit suicide you drink a lot of it and lie there and die. You don't do it a little at a time over a couple of days. And you don't stick a cross with the substance in your mouth after you die."

"A what?" she says.

The little tech holds up a plastic evidence bag with the blue plastic cross in it.

"Fuck me. That was in his mouth?"

"Well, we have to take your investigator's word for that because he removed it before we got here. But if it was, it was placed in there post mortem. He wouldn't have been able to put it in and keep it in his mouth while he was still alive. Because of the seizures and vomiting. And by the way we found evidence of his vomiting in various locations around the building."

She shakes her head. "So he was murdered."

I nod. "By a killer who wanted him to suffer," I say. "And who left something significant behind in the body."

"Do we know what he put the antifreeze in yet?" she asks.

The little tech shakes his head. "We've gathered all the drinks and unpackaged foods to test. Hopefully, we'll be able to identify it. But . . . it may not even be here. The killer could've given it to him somewhere else or taken it with him when he left. We know he was here after the victim died."

8

"This whole thing gives me the creeps," Reggie is saying.

We are standing near her car outside Andrew's home. Everyone else is gone.

"It's weird that an ex-priest lives in an old church, and that he kept most of it as a church, right? It's odd at the least. Then for him to be murdered in it and that little cross to be shoved in his mouth. It's not just me, is it? It's bizarre."

I nod. "It's bizarre."

"And for his dog to be missing . . . It's just all so strange."

I don't say anything and we fall silent a moment.

Beneath the bright, hot October sun the traffic

coming into town on Highway 71 is light and relatively quiet as it breaks for the changing speed zone.

All is quiet in the large parking lot of Ake's Septic, but beyond it Ace is bustling.

"I know anyone can kill in any manner imaginable," she says, "but poisoning is usually a woman's weapon, is it not?"

"Not really," I say. "That's sort of a misconception. It may have been true at one time. I'm not really even sure about that. Statistically, women commit a lot less murder than men, but they use just as many weapons. Like men, they use guns more than anything else, but poison is way down on the list for them just like it is for men. The truth is poison just isn't used as a murder weapon much period. Seems like I recall it being used in something like one half of one percent of all murders. Women do use it more than men per capita but only by something like two percent."

"Oh, well, that just adds to how bizarre this all is, but I was wondering why we referred to the killer as *he* in there."

I nod. "I haven't ruled anyone in or out yet, and I'm certainly mindful that it could be a woman, but . . . statistically . . ."

"Yeah, I know."

"We all probably did it because we usually associate

Catholic priests with men instead of women for the most part. It's a highly patriarchal church."

"Aren't they all," she says. "It's a patriarchal world."

"You said that the 911 caller was male, and we know Andrew couldn't be seen from outside so the caller had to have been inside the church with him—like the killer was. *That* and the fact that he wouldn't give his name . . ."

"Makes you think the caller was the killer," she says. "And he was male so . . ."

"But I won't forget the killer could just as easily be female."

"Never thought you would," she says. "Was just asking for my own benefit."

"I appreciate the reminder," I say.

"So," she says. "What do you need? How do you want to work this?"

"Don't need anything for now," I say. "I'll keep doing the canvasing myself, gather as much information as I can while we're waiting for confirmation that it was ethylene glycol poisoning and what it was in. Then at that point I may need some help."

"Sounds good," she says. "How well did you know him?"

"Not well," I say. "But I've known him for a while. Worked with him in the prison system. He was more than an acquaintance, less than a close friend."

"Do you know why he left the priesthood?"

"Just what he said. That he was old and ready to retire."

"No scandal or—"

"Not that I know of," I say. "I don't think so."

"Did he drink?"

"No."

"Have a thing for little boys?"

"No."

"You sure?" she asks.

I nod. "Pretty sure. I'll look at every possible motive, but I'll be shocked if there's anything scandalous at all. I knew him to be a man of tremendous integrity and morals. A truly decent human being."

"And yet someone murdered him."

9

After Reggie leaves and before I head to my meeting at the prison, I sit in my car and search for information on poison being used in murder.

I can't help but think of how willingly, even eagerly, I used to pour poison into my own body, and I'm relieved again that, at least for now, alcohol is no longer the issue for me it once was.

The best data I can find is from the Federal Bureau of Investigation Supplemental Homicide Report.

Like all reports, it's incomplete and inaccurate for a lot of reasons related to how the information is reported, but it's by far the best.

I had told Reggie that men commit many more

murders than women, but I had forgotten just how many more it really is.

The male of the species commits 90 percent more murders than the female.

When men commit murder they use a gun to do it 67 percent of the time, followed by a knife at 12 percent, beating at 7 percent, and a blunt object at 4.5 percent. Poison joins strangulation, asphyxiation, fire, drowning, and explosives as each being less than a percent.

When women commit murder they use a gun 39 percent of the time. A knife 23 percent of the time. Beating 12 percent. A blunt object 5.4 percent. Asphyxiation 2.6 percent. And poison 2.5 percent of the time.

Father Andrew's killer is still much more likely to be a man but it could be a woman, and the fact that poison was used does increase the odds slightly that it could be a woman.

I need to go, but I take a few more minutes to research ethylene glycol poisoning before I do.

Poisoning by antifreeze is fairly common—both accidentally and intentionally—and not just among humans. It enters the body primarily through ingestion, and because of its sweet taste it often goes unnoticed. It's also because of its sweet taste that so many dogs and cats die from drinking antifreeze from leaking radiators or spilled bottles each year.

This type of poisoning can happen gradually over

several hours, and symptoms may not occur immediately. As the body absorbs the antifreeze, the chemical is converted into other toxic substances such as glycolaldehyde, glycolic acid, glyoxylic acid, acetone, and formaldehyde.

As it does the body slowly begins to react to the antifreeze in your system. The time required for the first symptom to appear depends on the amount of antifreeze ingested. The earliest symptoms can develop within half an hour to up to 12 hours, and can include feeling drunk or dizzy, headache, fatigue, lack of coordination, grogginess, slurred speech, nausea, and vomiting.

As the body continues to break down the antifreeze over the next several hours, the chemical begins to interfere with the functions of the kidneys, lungs, brain, and nervous system. Organ damage can occur 24 to 72 hours after ingestion. The symptoms include rapid breathing, an inability to urinate, rapid heartbeat, convulsions, and loss of consciousness.

Father Andrew did not have an easy death. Is that what his killer intended? Did he want him to suffer, to experience as much agony and indignity as possible? And if so, why?

10

I arrive at Gulf Correctional Institution just in time for my meeting in the Admin conference room.

The enormous wooden table is surrounded by department heads, all here to discuss the possibility that a hurricane that doesn't exist yet may make landfall near here sometime on Wednesday.

The warden is out of town, so the meeting is being conducted by the new assistant warden for operations.

"Okay people," he says. "I'll try to make this as brief as possible. I hate meetings as much as the rest of you."

His name is Hal Lew and he's a stout thirty-something white man in discount department store clothes and a military-style haircut. Until a month or so ago he had been in a CO uniform for fifteen years.

"Y'all know why we're here," he says. "The governor

has declared a state of emergency because that little low-pressure area from down in the Caribbean Sea is now officially a tropical storm and is expected to be a hurricane and is headed in this direction."

Several of the department heads around the table indicated they hadn't even heard about it yet.

"Y'all know how these things go," he says. "They got all these spaghetti models that show it coming up into the Gulf and hitting the Panhandle. As usual they got our asses in the damn cone of uncertainty. Chances are good we're good, but even if it comes in right on top of us what will we get? Little wind, little rain. Few hours later, beautiful blue skies again."

Bradley Myers, the librarian, a sixty-something black man in need of a haircut, clears his throat. "I'd be careful 'bout underestimating this one," he says. "It's been cooking for nearly a week already and right now the Gulf is unseasonably warm. This has the potential to get juiced into a real son of a bitch."

Lew nods. "Always that possibility, but as far inland as we are and as well constructed as our institution is . . . we'll be fine. But we've got to jump through these hoops, so . . ."

"I'm tellin' you," Myers says, "don't sleep on this one."

"How many times we all been through this?" Lew says. "It's always the same. Weathermen get worked up, government agencies make up a bunch of shit for poor bastards like us to have to do . . . and then nothing much happens. I've lived here my whole life and it's always the same."

"Until it's not," Myers says. "That's the trouble with so many near misses for so long. Makes us complacent. Lackadaisical. As in the days of Noah before the flood they were eating and drinking, marrying and giving in marriage, until the day that Noah entered into the ark, and they knew nothing until the flood came and carried them all away."

"*Biblical*?" Lew says. "You're gettin' fuckin' *biblical* about this shit? It's a tropical storm."

"Not for much longer."

"And isn't the Bible stuff *his* job?" he adds, nodding toward me. "The thing about hurricanes is that they can't sneak up on you. They're a slow-moving train wreck."

"That's true," Myers says, "but what does that matter if you in the path of the train? Besides, there's some indication this one's going to be a fast mover."

11

"We were cordial enough," Tad Yon is saying. "Not a lot of love lost between us but we didn't have any major problems neither. Certainly not happy he's dead or anything."

Tad Yon and his young family are or were Andrew's closest neighbors. He's a late-twenties city employee with sole custody of his kids and a girlfriend who just graduated from high school the previous spring.

We are standing out in his front yard with a good view of Andrew's place, which is directly adjacent.

"How'd he die?" he asks. "Was he killed? That why you're here? Any idea who did it?"

"I thought most people really liked Andrew," I say. "Was he not a good neighbor?"

He hesitates. "He was . . . fine. Like I said we didn't

have any big issues. We just weren't really neighborly like most people 'round here."

"Why's that?"

He shrugs. "Wasn't just one thing. More like lots of little things."

"Such as?"

"We weren't crazy about having that type of church over there to begin with, but we got used to it. And there were only people over there for a little while once a week. But then when it closed and a priest bought it to live in it . . . I don't know. That was just kind of odd. Who wants an ex-priest living in an ex-church as their neighbor?"

I nod and tell him I understand though I really don't.

We are quiet a beat. I can tell he's hoping we're done, but I wait, acting oblivious to the awkwardness.

Finally, I say, "Did y'all ever have any run-ins or—"

"Oh, nothing like that, no, sir. We mostly just kept our distance from each other."

"I can tell there's more," I say. "What did he do?"

"He didn't do anything. But he had that huge dog, you know? I have two small boys. That thing weighs more than double what they do put together. I told him to keep it away from my youngins. He didn't like it, but I'm their dad. It's my job to protect them. I take that seriously, you know?"

I nod.

"I told him if it ever came over here onto my property I'd shoot it. Should've seen the way he reacted."

"About like you would if he threatened to shoot one of your children if he came over onto his property?"

"They never would. They know better. Besides, it's a damn dog. It ain't the same. You sayin' it is?"

"I'm saying how it felt to him and why he reacted the way he did."

"Oh. Well . . . Yeah. I guess. I know some people are like that with their dogs. We've never had anything but yard dogs. I like 'ems good enough, but they ain't nothin' compared to my boys."

I nod and think about how he said the words *They never would. They know better.*

"Did what religion he was bother you?"

He shrugs. "Not especially. I mean, we don't believe in it or nothin' but . . ."

"You've got two small boys," I say.

"Yeah."

"And you hear all the reports of Catholic priests and what they do to little boys."

"Yeah."

"And your job is to protect them."

"It is."

"So it was really him you were telling to stay away," I say. "Not his dog."

He shrugs and sort of half nods. "I guess, yeah. But the dog too. Though she seemed sweet."

"Did Father Andrew ever do anything he shouldn't have toward your—"

"*No*. No. Nothing like that. But . . . I never gave him the chance to, now did I?"

"Have you ever heard any rumors about him?"

"No. He wouldn't still be living beside us if I had."

"Actually, he's not," I say.

"Huh?"

"He's not living beside you any longer, now is he?" I say.

12

"He didn't have a lot of visitors," Madison Smith is saying. "So the few he had stood out."

Tad's young live-in girlfriend has joined us, along with his two sons, who are playing with plastic Tonka trucks in a pile of dirt about twenty feet away.

Madison Smith looks even younger than she is—her flat-chested, petite body, stringy blond hair, slight over-bite, and the freckles flecking her unvarnished face conspire to make her look thirteen instead of eighteen, which makes her look even more like a Lolita and him even more like Woody Allen.

"Who were they?" I ask.

"If they went there," Tad says, "she can tell you. Maddy's like our neighborhood watch all by herself.

Truth is she can tell you anything happening in the entire town. Sheriff's department should put her on the payroll."

So his child-girlfriend is a bored busybody willing to gossip. That could prove useful.

"I have thought about maybe wanting to be a cop," she says, and I wonder if her thoughts are as convoluted as her words.

"If you ever decide you want to I might be able to help you with that," I say. "Especially if you can help us with this investigation."

"Radical," she says, and sucks her saliva from around her protruding top front teeth and swallows. "Like I said, he didn't get many. It's kinda sad, I guess. Unless . . . Anyway, there was—I guess unless he was a perv. Didn't need to be around anybody then, did he? 'Specially kids. Anyway . . . there was one woman who came over sometimes. She probably—nobody came much, but she probably came the most. She was an older woman, kinda grandma looking. At first I thought maybe they were . . . you know, doing it, but . . . then I got to thinking and I think she probably just felt bad for the old guy. What I think what it was . . . was that she was a—like she used to go to the church there when it was . . . back when it was open. Well I figure she's the—she might be the . . . have been the secretary or something like that and she's just checking on him because he like used to be a priest and that used to be a church and shit, you know?"

I nod.

"I don't know her name, but . . . I know what she looks like. I could find her on Facebook for you or something like that. Do like a Facebook lineup. Ever done one of them before?"

I have no idea why if she's just finding the lady on Facebook for me it would be a Facebook lineup but I just roll with it.

"No," I say, "you'd be the first."

"Co-oool," she says. "Hear that, Daddy? I'd be the first. Whatta you think about that?"

My stomach turns at hearing her call him *daddy*.

Tad beams proudly.

Ironic that they're so concerned that their neighbor might be a perv.

"Let me get your digits and I'll text you her name when I deduce her out," she says.

I really don't want her having my digits but I can't think of a good excuse not to give them to her. "This number is for official police business only, so—"

"Oh, don't worry. I would never give it out to anyone else. I'll be the only one to ever use it."

"And only for official police business," I say, "so just the lady who visited Father Andrew's name."

"Roger that," she says, giving me a thumbs-up. "Ten-four."

"Who else visited him?"

"Sometimes random poor people would stop by for handouts," she says, "thinking it was still a church or something maybe. I'm not sure. He'd always give them stuff. Mostly out of his garden. He'd always give the families with kids more."

She says this last like it's something highly suspicious.

"Almost like they had more mouths to feed?" I offer.

"Maybe, I guess, but I was thinking . . . you know . . . 'cause of kids. Always wondered if the kids had to do things to get the food."

"They didn't," I say. "Father Andrew wasn't a child molester."

"Well, that makes—I guess that makes sense 'cause they were never there long enough for anything like that to happen and he was never alone with them."

During this entire time neither Tad nor Madison have so much as glanced over at his two boys playing on the dirt pile.

The boys, who appear to be between five and seven, are playing with quiet intensity, but with the highway so close and no fence in the yard I'd be watching them far more closely—and would have even before I read *Pet Semetary*.

"Yesterday a young boy in a red shirt went over there

twice," she says. "Once like with the old man—like helping him back home 'cause he was drunk, I think, and once by himself."

"Was it a red Ace shirt?" I ask.

She nods slowly. "Coulda been."

That would make the *young boy* around the same age as her.

"How long did he stay?" I ask.

"Not long either time," she says.

"Any other visitors we need to know about?"

"I wouldn't call her a visitor, but . . . yeah . . . you need to look real close at his neighbor to the backside of his property."

I glance over at the old St. Lawrence building and the lot it sits on. There is no neighbor visible in the back, only woods.

"Can't see it from here," she says, "but the Epps family lives back there. There's like a barrier of woods between them, but they're there. They're the ones that gave or sold or whatever the property for the church to be built on. They're big time Catholics or were or whatever, but . . . they had a fallin' out over something and Jan Epps fuckin' hates—or hated, I guess—that old man. She didn't go over there a lot, but when she did it was with screeching tires and hollerin' and yellin' and cussin' and fussin'. Always made a big scene. One time she even fired a gun. The bitch is cra-cra. I told my Tad, she better not ever come over here actin' like that or I'a beat her ass bad and stomp a mud hole in her. I got some sure 'nough dog in me when I need to."

"What did I tell you?" Tad says. "Does my baby girl have the 411 or what? Her fine, tight ass is smart and tough and deductible like Sherlock fuckin' Holmes."

I realize *deductible* isn't what he means, but he's probably not as wrong as he seems. She probably qualifies him to take a child tax credit.

13

"He was a nice old guy," Marie Ann is saying. "Would always stop and pass the time of day if I was outside."

After finishing with Tad and Madison, I crossed Highway 71 to the old mobile home rental where I found Marie Ann Trainer in the fenced-in front yard.

"Seemed lonely," she is saying. "I felt bad for him. Tried to make a point to come out if I saw him. 'Course only when Little Ben wasn't around."

"Little Ben?"

"My son. Actually, it's his place. I'm just crashing with him while I look for a place of my own."

I'm not surprised she's having to crash with her son. That's not the only way in which she's crashing. She has all the signs of meth addiction—the emaciated body, the facial tics and body twitches, the skin sores, and, of course, meth mouth, the missing and rotting teeth that comes from poor nutrition and hygiene and the way the drug dries it out.

"Why did you have to wait until he wasn't around?"

"They have history," she says. "From before I moved in."

"Is Ben here?"

"Little Ben's at work," she says.

"Where does he work?"

"On a loggin' crew for Taunton Timber."

"Would you have him give me a call?" I ask, handing her my card.

"Sure," she says as she takes it and looks at it.

"What's the history between them?"

She shrugs. "Don't know all the details, but they got into a . . . altercation. Which was stupid for the old priest. Ben is so big and so strong and he's got a temper on him. Don't get me wrong . . . he's not a bad boy, you just don't want to back him into a corner, but . . . what man is that not true about, right?"

I nod. "What happened?"

"Like I said I don't know all the details."

"Just tell me the ones you know."

"Well . . . I don't know. You probably need to wait and talk to Little Ben."

"I'll talk to him but just tell me in general what happened."

"Little Ben used to have a little dog and no fence. The priest's dog—she was a big son of a bitch, I'll tell you—got loose and come over here and was hurtin' Little Ben's dog, Bud. Now to be fair and honest and all, I'm not sure if the priest's dog was just playing with Bud or was tryin' to kill him. She was so big and powerful and little Bud was so little, just a pup really. But be that as it may the big bitch was killin' little Bud. Well . . . Little Ben and the priest wound up in the yard about the same time. The priest come to get his dog and Ben come out to see what all the squealing was about. Well . . . the priest got his dog off of little Bud but it was already too late. Little Bud lie dying. Well . . . Little Ben started telling the old priest what a piece of shit he was to let his dog out to kill his dog and that he was going to beat his ass for him, and damn if that big bitch didn't break free and attack Little Ben. Knocked him on the ground and started mauling him like a damn bear. She was just protecting her master, but . . . she really hurt Little Ben. The priest got her off of him but the damage was done. She killed his dog and bit and scratched him all up. His heart was hurt about his little dog and his pride was hurt that the priest's dog kicked his ass, so . . . they don't speak. And if I have to choose a side it's Little Ben's, but the priest nor his dog didn't mean no harm and I feel bad for him."

"Has Little Ben been planning to get back at the priest?"

"That's just talk. He just talks. He's mouthy like his mama. Don't mean nothin' by it. Just our way of blowing off steam."

"Did Ben kill Mary?"

"Who?"

"The priest's dog," I say.

"No. No, not at all. Why would you even say something like that?"

"Because she's missing and you only referred to her in the past tense."

14

"You think it's possible Ben Trainer poisoned Andrew's dog with antifreeze," Reggie is saying, "then . . . Andrew killed himself or Ben poisoned him too?"

I'm on the phone with Reggie as I walk back across Highway 71 toward my car still parked at Andrew's. I've just given Reggie a brief account of what I got out of Marie Ann Trainer, Tad Yon, and Madison Smith.

"It's possible," I say.

"Of course, it could've been an accident," she says. "He poisons the dog then Andrew is poisoned by accident."

"Again, it's possible."

"He could've just poisoned him on purpose," she says.

"Andrew I mean. Maybe he poisoned Andrew and the dog drank some by accident."

"But wouldn't Mary be dead inside the church with Andrew?" I ask. "Why dispose of her body and leave Andrew's?"

"Maybe she went out into the woods behind St. Lawrence's to die."

"She wouldn't be able to if he died first, would she?" I say. "All the doors were closed."

"Yeah, you're probably right. Maybe Ben killed Mary, Andrew buried her, then killed himself. I don't know. I'm just tossing out ideas. It may not have anything to do with Ben or the dogs. Could be Tad thinking he was protecting his boys or any number of a thousand other people we don't even know about yet."

"True."

"It's early days," she says. "Something'll turn up. Where are you headed now?"

"To talk to the Epps," I say. "They live on the other side of the woods behind St. Lawrence's. Then back to Ace to interview the kid who walked Father Andrew home yesterday and went back to check on him."

"Huh?" she says, her mouth away from the phone slightly. "Hold on a minute, John."

A few moments later she comes back on the phone and says, "Go back to Ace first," she says.

"Why?"

"That's where the 911 call came from."

15

"Really?" Dawn Lister is saying.

We're in her office and I've just told her that the 911 call came from here at Ace. Out in the store a crime scene tech is dusting the phones for prints, while deputies do a search of the premises.

I nod. "Yeah."

"Wow."

"Any idea who may've made the call?" I ask.

She shakes her head, but I can tell she's thinking. "So many people in and out of here all the time."

"How many workers?"

"Including me and the other manager between five and seven most days," she says. "And we average over a hundred customers each day, but we're busiest in the mornings. Usually slows down around three. When was the call made?"

"8:09 this morning."

"So there were probably nearly twenty people in the store around then."

"How many phones?" I ask. "How accessible are they?"

"Eleven," she says.

"Wow," I say. "That's a lot."

"Yep. One in each of our three offices. One in the break room. One in the warehouse. One by the garden center door. One at the paint hub. One at the key hub. One in the mechanical closet. Two up front at the registers. All very accessible."

"Don't have to dial anything special to get an outside line?" I say. "Anyone could just pick any of them up and make a call?"

She nods. "And depending on where you did it you might not even be seen by anyone else. I mean if they were trying to make a quick call without being seen ... it's possible."

"Tell me about your surveillance system," I say.

"It's good," she says. "Very good. New store. New system. But ..."

"But?"

"It's designed to capture shoplifters not phone callers."

"So all eleven lines aren't on camera?"

"No."

"How many?"

"Let's go have a look," she says.

She stands up and walks out from behind her desk and leads me to the office next to hers where the large security monitor is mounted.

The TV looks to be about 70 inches and has 31 small live camera feeds showing on it. In addition to seeing customers and employees, the crime scene techs and deputies show up in several of the small video feeds.

"There are normally 32 feeds," she says, "but the camera on the side of the building is out, which means the warehouse phone isn't visible."

The office, which is mostly empty, has the same back wall of pine shiplap and a large desk. Obviously belonging to a Florida State football fan, the office is decorated with FSU memorabilia—including a football in a display case signed by coach Jimbo Fisher and a garnet and gold FSU spear like the one thrust into the fifty-yard line of the football field at Doak Campbell Stadium at the start of each game.

"The nice thing is you know what time the call was made," she says. "Means we won't have to wade through hours of footage."

"True, but could you start them around eight and let's watch them through about eleven after?"

"Yeah."

She sits at the desk and withdraws a purple mouse and black mousepad out of the drawer and begins moving the curser around and clicking buttons on the large monitor.

"We've got cameras on every aisle," she says. "They are mounted on the ceiling at each end and point down to cover the row up until about the main center aisle. Since there's not much on the center aisle and because it's so visible there aren't any cameras on it—though some of it is picked up by the other cameras. That means the key hub, which is in the center back, isn't visible. None of them are aimed at the phones specifically, but most of the phones can be seen in them—though some of them will be from a pretty good distance."

She moves the mouse around and clicks the buttons until she has the camera feeds all paused on 8:00 a.m.

"I can zoom in on any single camera feed that we need to," she says. "Let me show you the feeds with the phones."

She stands, walks over to the monitor, and points to the phones that can be seen in the small frozen frames.

"Here are the two at the cash register," she says. "Though unless it was an employee I doubt the caller used them. Here's the one at the paint hub. The wall next to the garden center door. And I think that's it."

I look at the frames she's pointed out.

The camera trained on the front registers and the phones beside them is the only one at an angle from directly overhead. The phone at the paint hub is surrounded by big bright displays of color in virtually every shade imaginable.

"That leaves these three offices back here," she says, "the break room, the key hub, the mechanical closet up front, and the warehouse."

"So seven that could've been used to make the call without being recorded," I say.

"Yep."

She takes a seat again and starts the feeds.

We watch as the footage rolls across each small window, seeing customers come and go, employees move about the store—fetching items, restocking shelves, carrying materials to the front, helping customers find what they're looking for.

When 8:08 rolls into 8:09 all the visible phone receivers are on their cradles.

"Well," she says. "We know none of these four phones were used to make the call because they weren't in use at all."

"So someone snuck into one of the offices, the break room, or the mechanical closet, or used the phone at the key hub or in the warehouse to make the call," I say. "Which means . . . either they are very lucky or they knew which phones are covered by the security cameras."

"Why call from here, I wonder?" Dawn says.

"It's close to the crime scene," I say. "Could've just walked over here after killing him. A cell phone would be traceable. And he could make the call from here with anonymity. We can trace the call to here but not to him. And if he used the warehouse phone he wouldn't have even had to come inside."

"True," she says, "but I'm just wondering if he has a connection to the store or was just looking for a place to make the call."

"That *is* the question," I say. "Do any of your employees have a connection to Andrew?"

She shrugs. "Not that I know of. But you can interview 'em and find out. You can even use one of our offices."

"You really are a helpful hardware folk."

She starts to stand, then stops. "You're welcome to interview everyone—and you probably will anyway, but . . . might not be a bad idea to look at the security footage again to see where everyone was. At least you'll know who wasn't making the call."

"That's a good point. I should've thought of that."

"Can't think of everything."

"How did you?"

She shrugs. "Read a lot of true crime books. Actually wanted to go into forensics at one point, but I had a baby instead. And I'm married to a crime novelist."

"Do you mind running it back and identifying everyone for me?" I say.

She shakes her head. "Not at all. You're keeping me from some paperwork I'm not anxious to do."

She works the purple mouse again and rewinds the footage to 8:08.

"Okay," she says. "That's Tiffany and LaTracy at the registers."

She points to two early twenties women, one white, one black, ringing up customers at the checkout counters.

"Neither one of them used the phones at 8:09 and both of them were at the registers from open until their lunch breaks."

She points to a middle-aged man restocking PVC fittings. "That's Lamar."

"You were right," I say. "This is very helpful. Thank you."

"No problem," she says. "I'm not saying you need to pay me back or anything, but if you wanted to you could let me shoot the killer once you catch him. I've always wanted to shoot somebody—at least in the leg."

"I'll see what I can do."

"That's Josh mixing paint," she says, pointing to a young man with blond curls spilling out of his Ace base-ball cap. "Alarua is with a customer in the garden center. See?" She points to a thick, butchy young woman with spiky platinum blond hair and thick workboots on loading bags of fertilizer onto a cart for a thin old lady beneath the shade cloth of the garden center. "I don't see anyone else on the feeds. The other manager is off today so that only leaves me—I'm pretty sure I was in my office —Levi, and Jenner. Levi is around nineteen or twenty. Works here full-time and attends Haney part-time."

Tom P. Haney Technical Center is the vocational school in Panama City.

"Jenner is a high school student," she says. "She works here part-time. She may already be gone for the day."

"That's okay," I say. "I want to start with Levi anyway."

16

L evi Tucker is a skinny but muscular boy with black hair, pale skin, and mesmerizing blue eyes. He's intense in the way of a certain type of teenage boy and alternates from too cool aloofness to mannered Southern gentility—both of which present as the affect of someone uncertain how to act.

"You helped Father Andrew home," I say, "and went back later to check on him?"

He nods. "Yeah, Miss Dawn told me the old guy was in pretty bad shape and would I mind walking him home. I didn't mind. I help with my grandfather sometimes. How we treat our elders says a lot about our character— as individuals and as a nation."

This last statement sounds insincere—more like

something he thinks he should say than something he genuinely believes.

"How was he when you walked him home?" I ask.

"Wobbly. I had to hold his arm to steady him. Said his abdomen was hurting. We had to stop twice for him to throw up. But he didn't want me to call an ambulance. Didn't want to go to the doctor. Just wanted to lay down. Said he'd be all right after some rest. He seemed better by the time we got there and got him in."

"Did you go inside with him?"

He nods. "Asked him where he wanted to go. Was hoping he wouldn't say the bedroom. He said would I mind helping him to the couch. So that's what I did. I went to the kitchen and got him a glass of water and made sure he had his phone. I stayed for a few minutes to make sure he was okay before I left. He seemed a little better, so I told him to call us if he needed anything else and I left."

"Was his dog with him?"

"The entire time," he says. "Never left his side. Was laying on the floor beside the couch as close to him as she could get when I left."

"Was anything out of place or suspicious in his house? Anyone there? Anything odd?"

He shakes his head.

"And you're sure you closed the door?" I ask.

He nods. "Positive."

"Did you lock it?"

He shrugs. "Not sure about that, but I made sure it was closed."

"What about when you went back later?"

"I guess I didn't lock it because I was able to go in without him opening the door for me. Anyway, Dawn asked if I'd go check on him. Said he wasn't answering his phone. Just wanted to make sure he was okay. I didn't mind. He was a cool old dude. I wanted to know that he was okay too. I knocked on the door, but he never came. Finally, I opened it and called for him. He didn't say anything but I could hear him snoring so I went into his little living room and . . . he was sound asleep on the couch—looked like he hadn't moved an inch. His dog was still lying on the floor right beside him. Didn't look like she had moved either. She raised her head, looked at me, then put it down again. Didn't bark or anything. So I crept back out and closed the door."

"And no one was there and nothing seemed out of place or—"

"Nothing. It was just like before."

"Happen to see anyone coming or going over there the day before that or earlier that day?"

"The older lady who always visited him," he says. "She might have been over there. Can't remember for sure, but it seems like maybe she was. Not too many days passed without her showing up over there."

"Any idea who she is?"

He shrugs. "Don't know her name, but she drives a big old white car. Has a hard time handling it. Can't park it for shit."

17

At her suggestion, Dawn Lister is present during my interview of Jenner Fields, and I'm glad she is because I'm not sure I would've been able to get her to answer any questions on my own.

Dawn had caught her just as she was leaving and asked her to hang around for a few minutes to talk to me—and though she had agreed, she's not doing much talking.

Before we called her in, Dawn had warned me how quiet and shy Jenner is, but she didn't do her justice.

All I've gotten from the pale, stringy blond, waif-like creature so far are nonverbal responses—mostly nods and shrugs.

Mercifully, Dawn steps in.

"Jenner, it's real important that you answer the questions, okay? Do you remember what you were doing this morning at a little after eight?"

She shrugs.

"Your timecard shows you clocked in at seven," Dawn says. "What did you do first thing? What were you doing a little over an hour later?"

She shrugs again.

"This is real important, Jenner," Dawn says. "Remember I asked you to scan the empties on the back left side of the store?" She turns to me. "Scanning empties or shooting the outs is what we call reordering. A worker takes a section of the store and goes aisle by aisle and uses the Eagle Mobile Device or gun to scan the UPC on the ends of any empty pegs."

I nod. "Is that what you were doing this morning?" I ask Jenner.

"Uh huh," she says to Dawn, as if she had asked the question.

"How long did you do that?" Dawn asks.

Jenner shrugs. "Not sure," she says, then after a long pause adds, "Most of the morning."

Her voice comes out in a low half-whisper, and I wonder if self-consciousness about it rather than shyness is why she says so little.

"What else did you do?" Dawn asks.

"Got called to help a customer a time or two," she

says. "Had to go clean the girls' bathroom. Covered the register for LaTracy to take her break."

Even though she's looking in Dawn's direction, she's still not making eye contact.

"And between each of those things you went back to scanning?" Dawn asks.

She nods. "Yes, ma'am."

"Thinking back to the first part of this morning," I say, "did you see anyone acting odd or suspicious?"

Continuing to face Dawn, she shakes her head.

"Did you see anyone go into the mechanical closet up front or use the phone at the key hub in the back?"

She shakes her head. "No. Sorry."

"Did you know Father Andrew?" I ask.

She shakes her head again.

"Ever go over to his house?"

She looks at me for the first time, her eyes widening, her head shaking vehemently. "No, sir."

"Do you know of anyone who has?" Dawn asks.

"Not that I know of," she says.

"Know anyone who doesn't like him or has had a run-in with him?"

Her pale face crinkles and it's obvious she does but doesn't want to say.

"Who?" I ask.

She twists her lips into a frown that makes her look even more like a little girl.

"It's important," Dawn says. "We won't say anything to anyone."

"I seen him and Levi almost come to blows once," she says. "Don't know why or what it was about. Heard Levi say he hated the old perv but . . . never really heard why."

18

"**D**o you want to talk to Levi again?" Dawn asks.

We have finished the interview with Jenner and have stepped back out into the store.

All around us customers are shopping—most of them leisurely, some with the help of workers in bright Ace T-shirts.

I shake my head. "Not right now. I'm sure I will but . . . I'll gather some more information and evidence first. What Jenner said about him was damning but it's just one person's word against another's. And she may have an ulterior motive for saying it."

"She *did* use to crush on him pretty hard and he never reciprocated it, so . . ."

I nod.

At the far end of the power tool aisle a guy catches my attention.

He is a young, heavily tattooed white man with unwashed hair, wearing jeans, work boots, and a wifebeater. But it's not his appearance so much as his manner that makes me notice him. His movements are furtive and self-conscious and generally suspicious.

As he stands there looking like he's about to steal a skill saw he is joined by two other men—one older, one about his same age, who act just as wrong as he does.

I can tell they're on Dawn's radar now too.

"You recognize them?" I ask her.

She shakes her head. "Not right, are they?"

"No, they're not," I say.

I'm about to walk over to them when the two crime scene techs come up.

"We're finished with the phones," the short brunette with the big brown eyes says.

"Give me just a minute," I say, and signal to Tony Harris, a deputy in the back, to join us.

"What's up?" he says when he reaches us.

He's a fresh young deputy, uncynical and still filled with more than his fair share of new-to-the-job enthusiasm.

"Would you do me a favor and keep an eye on these guys over here," I say, nodding toward the three men I've been watching. "And run their tag."

He nods. "You got it."

He heads over in their direction.

"Sorry about that," I say to the tech. "Go ahead."

"No problem," she says. "We've finished dusting the phones. Now we need to get the employees' prints for comparison and elimination."

"You can set up in the break room and I'll send the workers in one at a time," Dawn says. "I can go first."

"It's strictly voluntary," I say. "Make sure everyone knows we'd really appreciate their cooperation but they're free to refuse."

"And you want to know who refuses, don't you?" Dawn says.

I smile. "I just might."

I'm about to join the deputy over near the three suspicious men when I get a call from a deputy outside.

"Got something you need to see," he says.

"On my way."

I walk out the side door and around back to the large green Waste Pro dumpster.

I find a deputy named Davis inside the dumpster. As I get near him he stands up and says, "Lookie what I found."

He's holding a bright blue plastic bottle of Peak antifreeze in a gloved hand. It's obvious the 128-ounce container is empty, but it still has the bright red cap on it.

I nod.

"You don't seem particularly enthusiastic to see the murder weapon," he says.

I start to say something but he holds up the bottle so that the bottom is visible to me. And there in the thin, bright blue plastic is the cutout of a Roman cross.

19

"You had an eventful day," Anna is saying.

We are out for an evening stroll with our girls along Main Street. Johanna is leading the way on her little pink bicycle. Taylor is in a stroller, which I am pushing right behind her, and Anna and I, walking side by side, are bringing up the rear.

"A lot happened," I say, "but I didn't get anywhere much."

There is plenty I could be doing on the case, but we have both made a commitment to be home at a reasonable time so we can spend the evening with the girls before they go to bed. It's far easier some days than others, but it's not just a commitment but a priority for me. I truly cherish every second I have with my three girls.

"Probably got further along than you think," she says. "I'm so sorry to hear that Andrew is dead. What a sweet, kind old gentleman."

I nod. "It's a real loss for our little town."

In addition to having dinner together and reading a few chapters in a book to them every evening, we try to take them for a walk as often as we can. Strolling down Main Street of our small town not only does us tremendous physical, mental, and spiritual good, but it also gives us the chance to encounter so many of our friends and neighbors making their way back home at the completion of their day.

"I just can't imagine anyone wanting to hurt him," she says. "Got any idea on the motive? Was it love, lust, lucre, or loathing?"

"Unless it was for some small seemingly insignificant item that we've just missed, it wasn't robbery," I say. "Lots of valuables left behind—including cash—and as far we can tell nothing is missing."

"So not lucre. Could it be related to the church? Either generally like a hate crime or more specifically to do with him?"

"I hope to find out tomorrow," I say. "I'm interviewing a few people who should know."

"Tomorrow," she repeats. "Puts us one day closer to landfall." She looks around at the lovely, mild evening and says, "Doesn't look like a hurricane is about to hit, does it?"

"Never does," I say. "Some of the best, most beautiful weather we ever get is just before and especially just after one."

"Can't believe this one has happened so fast," she says. "We weren't even aware of it two days ago and in less than two days it'll be here."

When we first heard about the possibility of a hurricane hitting the Panhandle, it was going to be as a Category 1, maybe 2, and make landfall somewhere over near Destin or even farther west. Now, with less than 48 hours until it comes ashore, we're being told it will be at least a Category 3 and is far more likely to hit us directly.

"Was Andrew ever involved in any kind of scandal or . . . anything like that?" she asks.

I shake my head. "Not that I know of. I really don't think so."

"Wonder if it was to cover up another crime," she says. "Somebody could've confessed something to him and felt a lot less comfortable with him knowing now that he's not a priest."

"I hadn't thought of that," I say. "That's really good. Definitely something to consider."

"Any idea why he left the church?" she asks.

I shake my head. "I hope to find out tomorrow. It

could definitely be related to whatever the killer's reason was."

We wave to our neighbors passing by in their vehicles as we slowly traverse the uneven old sidewalk beneath the tall pines and enormous oaks, the sinking sun inching us out of dusk and into dark.

"As crazy as it sounds," I say, "it could be related to Mary, his dog. Seems to have had a fair amount of conflict surrounding her. And people have been killed for a lot less."

"A lot less," she says.

"It doesn't seem like rage," I say. "Particularly given the method. Seems pretty cold and calculating."

"Doesn't mean there's not a volcano of rage beneath."

"True," I say, adding, "The method of poisoning is one thing. Cutting out the cross and placing it in his mouth is another."

"Yeah, it really is," she says.

"Enough about my day," I say. "How was yours?"

"Not nearly as fascinating as yours," she says. "There's really nothing to tell. And there's nothing I need to talk about or process. You know I would if I needed to."

"Then let's talk about childcare and the storm," I say.

"The two very things I was going to suggest," she says. "Rudy was at Carla's when I picked up Taylor today. He was actually watching her and John Paul while Carla took a load of clothes to put on in the laundry building.

He seemed reasonably sober and she was just a few buildings away, but . . . I let her know that was not acceptable."

"No it's not," I say. "She can't sub out watching our daughter to anyone—especially a fall-down drunk without a parenting gene."

I then tell her about Carla calling that morning and how I found Rudy and how she wouldn't let me have him taken in.

"She swore to me that she would never let him keep them again—not even for five minutes," Anna says, "but I don't even like him being over there with them."

"Me either."

"Are we being overprotective?"

"I'm not sure there is such a thing with something like this," I say. "Their care and safety are our primary responsibilities. We didn't protect them from Chris and all the other dangerous and dark forces in the world just to turn them over to Rudy Pearson's drunk ass."

She smiles. "I agree. We may have to use Carla to watch them until we can find someone else, but we'll do it sparingly and keep a close eye on the whole situation."

I nod.

"Now," she says, "what do you want to do about the storm?"

"We have no idea where it's going to make landfall or how big it will be by then," I say, "but I'd like for us to prepare like it's going to hit us directly, which they're saying is a good possibility."

"Okay . . ."

"Given how warm the waters of the Gulf are it has the potential to intensify into something even more ferocious than what they're saying. If it comes anywhere close to us I'll be working the entire time—between the sheriff's department and the prison—and since we haven't protected our little angels from the forces of darkness just to put them in the path of a hurricane . . . would you be willing to take them to your folks?"

Anna's parents live in Dothan, Alabama, some ninety miles farther inland.

"You know I've never evacuated," she says. "Just like you."

Many North Floridians count it as a point of pride that they've never evacuated for a hurricane. This is especially true of those of us who live inland. Wewahitchka, Pottersville, and many of the other small towns around here are twenty or more miles inland, so even if our area takes a direct hit there are twenty miles of trees to slow the storm down and cause it to dissipate. The coast always takes the harder hit, and Anna and I tell ourselves that if we lived on the coast we would evacuate, and certainly now that we have children I believe that to be true. But inland or not the right storm will eventually hurt us all, and this may be the one. I suspect the prison librarian, Bradly Myers, is right. We've all grown complacent.

"I know," I say, "But—"

"I really hate the thought of being the little woman who evacuates while her brave strong man stays behind and takes care of everything."

"I know," I say, "but it's not like that and you know that. Like most things in our lives these days, this isn't about us. It's about our girls. Will you sacrifice your unblemished record of remaining for them?"

She nods. "You know I will," she says. "*Unless* . . . the storm takes a turn toward the west and there's no chance we'll be in it at all. It'll take some doing—scheduling and work wise—but for now I'd feel better about having them up there too. Just wish you could be with us."

My phone vibrates in my pocket and I pull it out and look at it.

"Sorry," I say. "I need to take this."

20

"You ou were right about those guys at Ace this afternoon," Tony Harris says.

He's the deputy I had asked to take a look at the three suspicious men in the hardware store earlier in the day.

"Thought you said—"

Earlier at the store today he had told me the plates came back clean.

"Van they were in *was* stolen after all," he says. "So was the credit card they used."

"But—"

"Neither was reported until just a few minutes ago," he says. "Old guy in Tallahassee. Doesn't drive anymore. Van was in a detached garage that he happened to go into this evening."

I glance at my watch. We had let the three men drive away in their stolen van nearly two hours ago.

"Have you already put out the BOLO?"

"Yes, sir."

"Didn't happen to see which direction they were headed in, did you?"

"No, sir. Sorry. And sorry for the fuckup."

"You did everything you could with the information you had," I say.

"Wish I woulda engaged with them more," he said. "More intel would help us right now."

"We'll find them," I say. "What did they buy at Ace?"

"A coupla chainsaws, shovels, axes, drills—like they plan to go all medieval on somebody's ass."

"Well, let's try to find them before they do."

"Yes, sir."

"Sorry about that," I say to Anna when I end the call.

"Daddy, stay off your phone," Johanna yells over her shoulder as she continues to make progress on her little pink bicycle.

"Yes, ma'am. Will do."

"Are we gonna get ice cream?" she asks.

"Yeah, ice cream," Taylor says, seconding the motion from the stroller.

"Should we put it to a vote?" Anna asks.

"I think we have to," I say.

"All in favor scream *ice cream*."

We all yell *ice cream*, the girls, taking their mom literally, screaming the words to the upper limit of their little vocal chords' capacity.

Brad Price pulls up next to the sidewalk in his emergency services vehicle, his round, tanned, bald head tilted, his mustache turned up above his smile, his eyes hidden behind his trademark dark shades. "I'm glad my window was down or you girls would've shattered it. What's all this racket about?"

"We're getting ice cream," Johanna says.

"Yeah," Taylor adds.

Short, thick, and muscular, Brad makes his living as a hero. An EMT and firefighter, and a truly likable guy who's friendly to everyone, he has as much love for our town and as much enthusiasm for its high school as anyone I've ever met.

"Y'all didn't hear?" he says, climbing out of his vehicle and closing the door. "The town's all out of ice cream."

"*Unh uh,*" Johanna says. "Mr. Brad you're so silly. And we wouldn't've broken your window either."

Johanna climbs down from her bicycle and begins to play with Taylor as we stand there and talk. As usual, they play together extremely well, Johanna's seven-year-old self part big sister part little mama to the three-year-old who couldn't be more her sister if they had the same biological parents.

"How's it going?" he says to me and Anna.

"You tell us," I say. "Any other emergencies besides the ice cream shortage?"

"I sure was sorry to hear about ol' Andrew," he says. "He was a good guy. Stuff like that's not supposed to happen in Wewa."

"No, it's not," Anna says.

"You figured out who did it yet?" he asks me.

"No," I say. "Where were you at the time of the murder?"

"Whenever it was I have an ironclad alibi."

"I figured you pulled up to confess," I say.

"No, but I have information related to the case for you. I'll tell you what it is if I get some ice cream too."

"I'll have to clear it with the sheriff," I say. "The department's policy is we don't pay for information."

Anna says, "I think you might be able to make an exception in this case."

"You remember Sally McBride?" he says.

I nod.

Sally McBride, the area's most notable animal whisperer, used to win every 4H competition we went to back when we were in school.

"She owns Bride and Grooming, that wedding themed pet place over in Callaway."

I nod. "Never used it because all we've ever had are yard dogs, but I've heard it's a huge success."

"Remember Petey Prescott?" he says. "We played football with him back in the day."

I nod.

"His daughter works for Sally."

"Okay . . ." I say, not sure where he's going.

"I'm about to connect the dots," he says. "Just give me a minute. Joan—that's Petey's daughter—she works at Bride and Grooming."

"You said that."

"I know. Hold on. She works over there but she lives over here."

"Next you'll be telling us she commutes," Anna says.

"Y'all're makin' me earn my damn ice cream, aren't you? She works over there but lives here *so* . . . sometimes she takes people's pets from over here with her to get groomed or brings supplies back for them. She's a sweet girl. Nothing like mean ol' Petey. Anyway, she has Mary— Andrew's dog. She's just getting back into town and wondering what to do with her."

"Brad solved the mystery of the missing dog," Anna says. "He definitely gets ice cream."

"*Mystery of the dog?*" Johanna says.

"Ice cream," Taylor says.

Neither looks at us, just continues to play with each other.

"Why don't you look happy about it?" Brad says to me.

"No, I am. I'm glad Mary's okay. I was just . . . I had

been thinking maybe Mary's disappearance had something to do with Andrew's death. Now that I know it doesn't, I have to rethink a few things."

"Well, you holla if you need my help," Brad says. "I solved one mystery. I don't mind solving another."

"I guess I need to call animal control," I say.

"I was thinking y'all could just take her home with you," Brad says. "Have something besides a yard dog for once in your lives."

"That'd be like having a bear, not a dog," Anna says.

"So is that a *yes*?" Brad says. "Should I tell Joan to drop Mary Bear off here?"

As if on cue, Joan Prescott pulls up in her newish stonewashed-blue Beetle convertible, the top down, Mary looking like an adult passenger in the seat next to her.

"Stay, Mary," she says as she gets out and walks over to us.

Both girls light up at the sight of Mary, but don't move toward her, just stare with wide-eyed wonder from where they are.

Joan, an eighteen- or nineteen-year-old in cool, colorful clothes, her shoulder-length brown hair wrapped in a tie-dyed bandana, looks like the kind of young woman who would drive a stonewashed-blue Beetle convertible with a mastiff in the front seat.

"Jordans," she says. "Uncle Brad."

She has called him *uncle* since he pulled her from her mangled, wrecked car not too long ago.

Her skin is as darkly tanned as Brad's, which really causes her clear blue eyes and bright white teeth to pop.

"Hey Joan," Anna says. "How are you?"

"Bummed about Father Andrew," she says. "Still just can't believe it. It seems surreal. I'm sure y'all'll think this sounds silly, but I really hate it for Mary too. She can tell something's not right."

Anna says, "We were just saying probably the best thing for her is to live with Brad."

"Can we come and visit her Mr. Brad?" Johanna asks.

"Yeah," Taylor says.

Anna says, "We're just teasing Mr. Brad. Mary's really not going to go live with him."

"Bummer, dude," Johanna says.

Brad lets out a loud burst of laughter and Johanna's cheeks blush crimson.

"He thinks you're very cute," I say to her.

"Yes, I do," he says. "The cutest. Maybe I'll take Mary just so you'll come and visit."

I look at Joan. "What do you think we should do with her?"

"I hate to see her go to the pound," she says. "And she's so big and Andrew never really socialized her much, so it's hard to imagine anyone would adopt her. I can't bear the thought of her being put down. I don't mind taking her—either temporarily or permanently."

"Are you sure?" I ask.

"Your dad won't mind?" Anna says.

Brad laughs. "Ol' Petey is with her like y'all are with your girls. She can have ice cream or anything else she wants anytime she wants it. Who you think got her that new car?"

"He's only helping," she says. "I'm gainfully employed —whatever that means. 'Sides . . . insurance from my other car mostly paid for this one anyway."

Brad nods. "She was in a hellacious wreck that almost took her out."

"Wouldn't be here if it weren't for Uncle Brad," she says to us. "Saved my life. Anyway, I don't mind taking Mary. Not at all. And Dad won't mind either. I'll probably take her to work with me every day for a while so she's not alone at the house and where she can learn to socialize with other animals and people."

"I'll have to clear it with Reggie," I say, "but if you're sure . . . I'm sure it would be best for Mary."

"You sure your dad won't mind?" Anna asks.

"I'm sure. He'll wind up falling in love with her. And he'll get a break when she goes to sleepovers at Uncle Brad's every few nights."

"When did you get Mary from Andrew?" I ask. "How did he seem?"

"I was supposed to get her this morning," she says. "That's what I usually do—just take them over during my shift, but—"

"*Them?*" Anna asks.

"I do this for a few different pets," she says. "Take them over with me for the day and bring them back when I get off in the evening. Saves some of the pet owners a trip over to PC. I'm going anyway and I enjoy the company."

She doesn't say anything after that so I prompt her.

"But this time was different?" I ask.

"Oh, yeah. Sorry. Andrew said he wasn't feeling well and would I mind going ahead and getting her. So when I got back into town and dropped off Sandy Strickland's poodle, I went by and picked up Mary. She spent the night with us last night and I took her with me this morning. That's why I don't mind taking her in. We've had a practice run. I could tell Andrew didn't feel good—sort of pale and clammy—said his stomach hurt, that he thought he must have eaten something bad, but he seemed okay. I thought maybe he was drunk or hungover but I didn't smell any booze on him. I don't even know if he drank."

"You remember about what time that was?" I ask.

"Probably about a quarter after six," she says. "I was home by six thirty."

"See anything suspicious or anyone else around when you—"

"Oh, wait. There was . . . An older lady in a big white car pulled in and parked as I was leaving. I see her around town some but I'm not sure of her name."

"That's Miss Peggy Munn," Brad says. "Everybody says she and ol' Andrew were an item."

21

"He was the most kind and gentle man I ever met," Peggy Munn is saying, continuing to sniffle and wipe at tears as she does.

It's the next morning—a Tuesday, just over 24 hours until Hurricane Michael hits us hard—and Peggy and I are at Andrew's.

I asked her to meet me here to talk so she could take a look around to see if anything is missing or out of place.

We have completed our walkthrough of the old St. Lawrence Catholic Church building and are now standing out back near Andrew's garden.

"Such a special soul," she says. "You know how much more beautiful someone is that doesn't know they're beautiful—or at least isn't conscious of it or self-conscious about it?"

I nod.

"That's the way it was with Father Andrew. He was gentle and kind and compassionate and good all the way down to his marrow, but he never thought about it, never advertised it, was never even conscious about it. It's just who he was. No affect. No pretense. No desire for anyone to notice. Just was. He was very Zen-like in that way."

I nod again.

She daubs at the corners of her eyes with the tissue that has been in her hand since she arrived.

She is a small, seventy-something woman with short gray hair, a stiff, straight back, and a careful, dignified bearing. Her hair and makeup are always impeccable and she's always dressed like she's on the way to church. Today she is in a white blouse with a frilly collar and salmon slacks that, because she is so short waisted, appear to come up to her breasts.

"You knew him," she says. "You know what I mean, don't you?"

"I do," I say. "I knew him to be a very good man and extremely humble about it. But obviously I wasn't nearly as close to him as you were. I'm not sure anyone was."

She smiles. "I was closer to him than just about anybody but Mary. She was his closest companion, his true love."

I start to say something but decide to wait instead to see what she says next.

"I still can't believe he's gone," she says. "It's not real. It can't be. And . . . to . . . be . . . killed. Why? Why would anyone want to . . . kill such a wonderful man?"

The occasional tears turn into a steady stream for a moment and she wipes her eyes and blows her nose with the little tissue held in her misshapen and wrinkled fingers.

"Can you think of any reason?" I ask. "Or anyone who might have wanted to?"

The day is unseasonably warm—even for early October in North Florida—and it makes me think of how warm the Gulf is and how it's the perfect pressure cooker to intensify hurricanes.

"No. Absolutely not. Father Andrew didn't have an enemy in the entire world."

Evidently my expression expresses my dubiousness.

"I know what you're thinking," she says.

"You do?"

"I bet I do. You're thinking that I'm saying all this because I'm infatuated with him, that he was my lover and now that he is dead I'm not remembering any of the bad about him, only the good."

I smile. "You might have a future in mind reading," I say.

"Don't have much of a future in anything at my age," she says. "And yes, I am in love with Andrew. I can't say *was* yet. Not yet. I have been for a long time. Will be as long as I live. But we weren't lovers. I'm married—not happily, but married. I would have committed adultery with Andrew or I would have left my husband in a heartbeat, but . . . he wouldn't dream of it. He . . . he said he felt the way about me that I did him, but that he couldn't do either one of those things because of the immorality and the scandal. I'm telling you . . . he was a truly good man. I know he had his faults, but they were normal human personality quirks and not character defects. The reason I say I can't imagine anyone wanting to kill him is even though he had strong convictions, he never made a show of them, never tried to make anyone else feel bad. It just wasn't in his nature. He was gentle above all else."

Andrew's garden looks like it needs water, and I make a mental note to turn on the sprinkler before I leave.

"So you can't imagine anyone wanting to kill him," I say.

"I really can't," she says. "And I don't think I'm being naive or blind. I mean . . . obviously someone did kill him, but I can't see it being about him or something he did."

"What do you mean?"

"Well, if you're walking along the street in New York City and get mugged and murdered . . . that's not really because of who you are or something you did per se. I'm saying it's got to be more about robbery or something than revenge."

"But you said nothing's missing, right?"

"I'm not saying it has to be robbery, just something impersonal like that. I don't know. I don't understand anything about this. And I'm sure I'm not thinking straight."

"You were here a lot, weren't you?"

"A couple of times a week, I'd say. I used to care for the church, take care of the books and the building. Now I just take care of Andrew. Or I did. I'd bring him food, help with his laundry. Any excuse to see him."

"So you'd know if something was missing or out of place."

"Oh, yeah, and the truth is he didn't have much for anyone to take. I'm just so glad Mary was with Joan when it happened. So grateful nothing happened to her. And that he didn't have to worry about her while it was happening."

"And no one was closer to him than you?" I ask.

She nods. "Don't think it was even close. I'm not sure who would even be second."

"So if he was being threatened or having conflict with someone, you'd know."

"I would. And he wasn't."

"Okay," I say. "If—"

"Could it have been an accident?" she asks.

"I guess it's possible," I say. "Though with certain elements of the crime it'd be hard to see how. Is there a chance it could be self-inflicted? Did he ask Joan to take Mary because he planned to end his own life?"

She shakes her head vehemently. "No way. He would never. He wasn't suicidal. Not in any way. And he wouldn't commit a mortal sin. And that's not just me not wanting it to be true. I assure you. And that's not just a loved one in denial."

"Was your husband jealous of Andrew?" I ask.

She laughs and shakes her head. "He's clueless. He still thinks the church is open and that I'm still taking care of it. He thinks religion is silly and never had anything to do with it. But I don't think he'd care anyway —I mean about me and Andrew. We lead very separate lives. As long as his supper's on the table and he's got clean drawers to put on he's happy."

"Do you know why Andrew left the priesthood?"

"No, not really, not completely, but you already know the person who can tell you for sure. I don't know if he will or not but Father Francis certainly could."

22

"In a lot of ways he was like a father to me," Father Francis O'Brian is saying.

"I'm so sorry for your loss," I say.

Father Francis is the pastor at St. Dominic in Panama City. We are speaking by phone as I drive over to Jan Epps's place. He's a late-fifties white man transplanted to Panama City from Chicago.

"The ideal father for an adult child really," he continues. "Always there when I needed him, never intrusive, never overstepped his bounds, only gave me input and advice when I asked for it. I lost my father when I was young and . . . and though it was years later and I was well into middle age, Father Andrew became the closest thing to a father I had since my own dad died."

I nod, then realize he can't see that so I say, "Yeah, he

really was one of the wisest and least forceful men I've ever met."

"I can't fathom anybody wanting to kill him," he says.

"Everyone keeps saying that," I say. "I feel the same way, but . . . you knew him better than I did and knew him in a way that no one else did—not even Peggy Munn. Can you think of any reason at all—no matter how small seeming?"

He is silent for a moment, eventually saying, "I truly can't. Think of the best person you know, the meekest and mildest, and imagine hearing that they were murdered. You'd be shocked and you'd have no idea who could've done it. You'd just know it wasn't because of something they did."

"Nothing related to the church or political or social issues?" I say.

"He wasn't exactly known for ruffling feathers," he says. "As far as I know he was at peace with everyone."

"Could it have anything to do with why he left the church?"

"I can't imagine," he says. "No one else really knew why he did. He didn't make a show of it. He never made a show of anything. It was all very quiet. I mean, I guess it's possible someone took umbrage just with the fact of him leaving, but . . . hard to see that leading to murder."

"Maybe if they thought he was defiling the church," I

say. "Not only by leaving it, but by living in a former church building."

"Sure," he says. "I could certainly see a crazed zealot doing something like that—especially if they thought he was having an affair with Peggy, but . . . they'd be wrong about all of it. Andrew never broke his vows while he was a priest and he actually continued to keep them even after he wasn't any longer."

I think about what he has said and we fall silent a moment as I turn onto the side road that leads to Jan Epps's place.

"I guess it's possible that it's a general hate crime against Catholic priests and not specifically to do with Andrew," he says. "About all that's reported about us these days has to do with child sex abuse. Someone could've thought they were taking out a pedophile." He pauses a moment then adds, "That would be ironic."

"Why's that?" I ask.

"Just because he was so repulsed by it and tried in his soft and gentle way to get more to be done about it," he says. "And because . . . that was the main reason he left the church."

"It was?"

"Yeah. I mean he was tired and he wanted a more solitary life but, yeah the main reason was he didn't think the church was doing enough to stamp out the epidemic. He worked on it from within but . . . at a certain point he just became too frustrated with the leadership not doing enough about it. And I get it. I do. I may be there soon myself. But even with that, even with him feeling so strongly that the most innocent of angels in our care were being victimized and exploited, he didn't give that as a reason for his retirement, didn't say a word about it. Didn't make a show. Just quietly retired. Hard to see how taking that approach would lead to anyone wanting to kill him."

"And yet someone did," I say.

23

Jan Epps meets me as I'm getting out of my car at the end of her long, winding driveway.

She is a small, rigid woman of indeterminate age—possibly somewhere between thirty-five and fifty-five—with short, thick dark hair but in the least fashionable or flattering style the salon had available, a plain, pale face, and small green eyes behind glasses that are both too big for her face and just too big.

The enormous white brick home behind her makes her appear even more diminutive, like a child who has put on her mom's matronly clothes and old glasses and is playing house with a mansion.

The intricately detailed and excessively large crucifix hanging from her neck causes Jesus to bounce around between her too-big-for-her-body breasts.

"I apologize, Detective," she says as she extends her small, cold hand, "but I have even less time than I thought I did, so I think it best we dive right in right here so we can both be on our way."

"If it'd be more convenient for you," I say, "you can come down to the station later today. Or we could meet at the substation."

"I feel certain we can cover everything here and now," she says. "Especially since I don't know anything. But if we run out of time, we can set up another time for us to talk. My attorney has a very comfortable conference room we could use. He'd probably want to be there anyway."

I smile and nod. First round goes to Jan.

The Epps's wannabe mansion looks to be a remodel in which a typical two-story house built in the seventies around here, probably by Mennonites out of Blountstown, was transformed into something resembling a home found on an Antebellum plantation, its facade all pillars and porches.

"Okay," I say. "Well, I won't waste any more time. We'll see how many questions we can get through right here. I understand that St. Lawrence's was built on your property."

"Is that a question?"

"It was a statement in search of confirmation."

"Yes, it was," she says. "Well, no. I guess, actually it

wasn't. The property ceased to be mine when I donated it to the diocese. But, yes, it was originally property God had blessed me with and made me steward over."

"And you gave it to the diocese with the understanding that a church would be built on it?"

She nods. "I did."

"And did you attend there?"

"For a while," she says. "Back when it first opened."

"Why'd you stop?"

"That's a personal and highly impertinent question," she says, "but I'm going to answer it anyway. I just want you to know I know how rude it is. I stopped attending St. Lawrence because I found Father Andrew to be a weak, mealymouthed man with no fire in his bones for the gospel of our Lord Jesus Christ and no true love or devotion for our holy church."

"You must have been so disappointed that after donating the land and finally getting a Catholic church here in walking distance from your house to not care for the priest."

"I not only donated the land, but most of the funds to build the building," she says. "And disappointment is an understatement, which is why I poisoned him years later."

"It's one thing to have a man who you felt that way about as the pastor of your church," I say, "but it's another to see it closed down and him actually buy it and live in it."

"And profane it," she says. "Which is why he had to be put down."

I know she's trying to bait me by her sarcastic confessions but she says them with such straight-faced earnestness I have to wonder if something about them is real.

"Just in the short time I've been around you," I say, "I get the sense that you would be the kind of woman who would put a clause in the contract that says if the church ever decided to close St. Lawrence you'd get the land and building back."

"I would never place a gift to God on his holy altar only to take it back," she says. "I would never want to offend the Lord God in such a way."

"So instead . . ."

"We get the abomination of that pathetic excuse for a priest and a man actually living in that sacred place with that big slobbering beast."

"Which is why you killed him?" I say.

"Right," she says. "Nodding."

I nod and look over her to the woods, beyond which is St. Lawrence.

"Just out of curiosity . . ." she says.

"Yeah?"

"If I really did decide to make a sacrifice to God out of

that measly man," she says, "do you think you'd be able to catch me, to find enough evidence to prove I did it?"

"I know what your answer is," I say.

"I want to know yours."

"I don't know," I say. "I've worked plenty of cases that couldn't be proved. A smart, disciplined, remorseless killer is extremely difficult to catch."

"But I bet you still think you'd catch me."

I smile. "Yeah," I say, nodding slowly, "I do."

"And yet you have unsolved or unproved cases," she says.

"Both."

"How do you handle them?"

"Not well. They keep me up nights."

"So you have unsolved cases but you think you'd be able to solve mine, so my implication does it follow that you think those other killers are smarter than me, better at planning and executing the, ah, deed?"

I shake my head. "Lots of factors involved in making a case. I'd never think something like that."

She allows herself a little twist of her thin lips that might have been something approaching a smile. "I'm not sure I believe you. But no matter. I did not kill Andrew. I don't know who did. And I had nothing to do with it. Murder is a sin—one of only a few to make both lists, the Ten Commandments and the seven deadly."

"Most of the people who commit murder know it's wrong and do it anyway," I say.

"I'm not most people," she says. "And I don't do wrong. I'm a serious servant of the Almighty and do my best to honor Him in thought, word, and deed. As a general rule I don't sin and when I do I repent, confess, and walk in God's forgiveness."

"Did you ever confess to Father Andrew?"

"The impertinence of your questions is truly stunning. You think a murder investigation gives you a free pass for rude behavior, don't you? No, I never made the mistake of confessing to that pitiful excuse for a priest."

"Have you been to confession since you killed him?" I ask. "Or are you walking around with that dark mark on your soul?"

"It was mildly amusing when I casually tossed into the conversation that I had killed him—particularly given that I'm speaking with the lead investigator on the case. It just doesn't work the same when you do it."

"When is the last time you've been to confession?" I say. "Who knows your secrets?"

"I have none," she says. "Is that all? I really need to get going if you'll excuse me. I'm—"

"Is that a path?" I ask, pointing to a narrow clearing in the woods behind her house.

"It is."

"Where does it lead?"

"I suspect you know," she says. "It leads through the woods to St. Lawrence."

"Mind if I take a little stroll on it?"

"It's private property," she says, "so don't make a habit of it, but sure, knock yourself out. Just be careful. There could be a killer out there."

24

"Don't believe a word that lying cunt says," Melissa Epps is saying. "She wouldn't know the truth if it sauntered up and bit her in her big giant tits."

Melissa Epps, Jan's stepdaughter, is an angry seventeen-year-old with straight shoulder-length hair dyed so black it has a blue tint. It's pulled back in a high ponytail and swings about as we walk through the woods between the Epps's place and St. Lawrence.

I encountered Melissa shortly after entering the woods, finding her lying on a fallen tree reading a beat-up old paperback copy of *The Virgin Suicides*.

Her long, lanky boy-body is sheathed in a pair of ripped and torn army-green fatigues, knee-high leather lace-up motorcycle boots, and a beige wifebeater under which there is no bra and through which no breasts or nipples protrude.

She has heavy dark eyeliner, short black fingernails, and her pale white skin bears a lot of black ink.

When I told her what I was doing back here and asked if I could ask her a few questions, she had offered to walk through the woods to Andrew's with me.

I smile and ask in a light tone, "So how would you characterize your relationship with your stepmom, Melissa?"

"Hostile," she says. "Aggressive—outwardly on my part, passively on hers. Contentious. But mostly nonexistent. We avoid interacting as much as we possibly can. She's a hateful, mean, spiteful, sour, repressed ol' cow. She uses religion to justify all her evil actions. She's controlling. Cruel. And petty. Whatever she told you, you can pretty much believe the opposite. She's a pathological lying cunt."

I just listen as we walk along the narrow trail, saving my questions until she's talked out and told me everything she has to.

I haven't been this close for this long to a teenager since I worked the shooting at Pottersville High, but being here with Melissa like this brings it all back to me —not that it's ever very far away, and I'm suddenly haunted by Derek and the others as if I'm walking through a graveyard instead of a forest.

Above us a canopy of oak and pine provide intermittent shade and dapple the forest floor beneath. In the late summer that early October is in North Florida, the understory encroaching on the tiny trail is rich and thick and verdant and smells slightly of vanilla and honeysuckle.

"I'm sure you're not gonna believe anything I say, but . . . if she weren't so lazy and morally opposed to doing anything for herself, I'd say she killed that sweet old man. She hated him. I mean *really*. Like loathed. Called him a false prophet and an anti-Christ. And hell, who knows . . . if the killing didn't require too much exertion maybe she *did* do it herself."

"Is your dad—"

"A weak panty waste?" she says. "Yes. Yes, he is. Jan had nothing when they met. He already owned all this—the house, the land. Everything we'd ever need. Before the ink is even dry on their marriage license she is wreaking havoc. Takes charge of everything like it's hers. She didn't even ask Dad if she could cut out that piece of land and give it to the church. It was supposed to be for my place one day. Dad travels a lot for work, but even if he were around more she'd still do whatever the fuck her crazy ass wants to and he wouldn't say a thing. She's all *God this* and *God that* but what she really worships is mammon. She's the most greedy and self-centered cunt I've ever met."

I want to ask her if she just learned that word, but don't want to distract her or cause her to stop talking.

"I know it bothered her that they closed the church down and that they didn't give it back to her, but I think there was more to it than that. I'm telling you . . . her level of hatred was because of more than just that. I bet she came on to Andrew and he shut her down. It has that level of vitriol."

I want to compliment her on her vocabulary and ask her how much time she spends reading but I don't want to distract her or cause her to stop talking.

"'Course if she did it wouldn't have been about sex. She's far too uptight to enjoy sex. No, it would've been about control, power, dominance. I bet it's a frozen lake down there. You know, where her cunt's supposed to be. I don't know. Don't want to know. But I tell you what I do know. I know that that lying piece of dried-up . . . said that Andrew's days were numbered and that she was going to get her property back—and this was weeks before he died."

"How well did you know Father Andrew?" I ask. "How often did you see him?"

She shrugs. "Not very well. I mean, well enough to speak if I saw him, but I hardly ever saw him. Sometimes when he was out for a walk. Occasionally when I had to return Mary. Always seemed like a pretty cool old guy.

Never got any creep vibe from him or any of the superiority or condemnation Jan flings about."

"You ever been in his house?" I ask.

She shakes her head. "Not since it was his house. I was made to go to mass there when I was younger, back when Jan was still trying to get us to look like a sainted happy family, but—"

She stops suddenly and looks down.

"*Ahhhh*," she says. "Look. It's one of Mary's paw prints. She used to come down this path to our house sometimes when she got loose. I miss her already. I tried my best to catch her and keep her away from that lying fuckin' cunt face if I could. She said she was going to put her down if she ever caught her on our property again. Said just a little bit of antifreeze would do the trick. Said dogs love the taste. Can you believe that? Who the hell says shit like that? I'll tell you who . . . monsters."

Eventually, we reach the back of St. Lawrence and Andrew's garden.

"He tried to give us vegetables he'd grown," she says. "One time Dad made the near fatal error of taking some when Jan wasn't around. I thought she was going to cut off his balls and cook them with the collard greens and make him eat them. But . . . she'd already taken them years ago, so . . . she couldn't do that."

"In a small town like this," I say, "there aren't many secrets, are there? You hear things. Sometimes they're not true. Sometimes they're partially true. Sometimes they're completely fabricated—just small-town talk."

She nods. She knows what I'm talking about. "Lot of stuff gets talked about at the high school," she says. "Between the students and the faculty. Lots of wagging tongues all close together."

"Ever hear anything about Father Andrew?" I ask. "Anything at all?"

She shakes her head. "Not a peep. I think he was genuinely righteous. But also . . . he just wasn't involved in the community anymore, you know? Besides seeing him walk his dog . . . He didn't do anything else, did he?"

"So you never heard anything at all?"

"Nothing."

We are quiet for a moment, looking at Andrew's garden and the back of his church house.

"Seems like a pretty sad little life," she says eventually. "But maybe . . . ultimately . . . they all are."

25

I meet Jessica Young at the Lunch Box for a quick bite and to go over the autopsy and forensics results so far.

The Lunch Box is actually a carnival food trailer with bright blinking lights and colorful signs that say things like Funnel Cakes, Ice Cream, Shakes, Nachos, and Onion Rings, parked in the old Wewa Hardware parking lot at the end of the road we live on. An Easy-up tent behind it with a picnic table beneath it serves as the only place to eat for the mostly to-go establishment.

"It's like there's a carnival in your neighborhood," Jessica is saying.

I smile. We are sitting at the picnic table under the blue-and-gree awning and surrounded by large plastic colorful cartoon characters—a Yogi Bear knockoff is waving at us, next to a bright yellow lion whose cavernous mouth yawns wide open—less than one hundred yards from our home.

"The girls love it," I say. "Want to get ice cream every night after we walk."

"And I bet y'all do," she says.

I laugh. "We get it pretty often."

"Y'all are such a good little family," she says. "Love how you and Anna love each other and how y'all are with the girls. Such a good example. And it gives us single ladies some hope."

"That's very sweet, Jessica," I say. "Thank you."

From inside the trailer the cashier signals that our food is ready and I jump up and retrieve it.

When the carnival trailer was parked here and became semi-permanent the menu changed somewhat. Now it's mostly hamburgers, hotdogs, Philly cheesesteaks, and french fries, with the more carny fare saved for Funnel Cake Fridays. I have a cheeseburger with everything but pickles and she has a Philly loaded with peppers and onions and a side of fries.

"Mind if I go over this while we eat?" she asks, nodding toward the open file folder on the table next to her food, her phone atop it keeping the pages from blowing away in the breeze.

"I'd prefer it," I say.

"Autopsy confirms what we suspected," she says.

"Kidney tissue revealed traces of calcium oxylate crystals. Won't be official until we get the lab results back, but they will say the same thing. He died of ethylene glycol poisoning."

"Any idea how long it took to kill him?" I ask.

"Probably a couple of days," she says. "No more than three. Maybe less. He probably continued to take the poison during that time period."

"He took it more than once?"

She nods. "Think so."

"Do you know what it was in?"

She nods as she glances down at the papers beneath her phone, taking a quick bite of her steak sandwich as she does. "It was in the orange juice in his fridge."

I think about that for a moment.

"It wouldn't take much and he may have not even tasted it or he may've thought the juice tasted extra sweet. It was a new carton and a lot of it was gone. He probably just kept drinking it, hoping it would help him feel better or fight off whatever bug he had."

"I'm not sure if the killer would even care," I say, "but since Andrew lived alone he wouldn't have to worry about someone else drinking the juice."

"Exactly. I mean, it was still a bit of a risk. Andrew could've had company and offered them something to drink."

I nod. "Yeah, he had to know there was good chance

that Peggy Munn would stop by. Of course, he could've wanted to kill her too—or at least not minded. Or it could've been her that put it in there."

"The techs found an identical carton of juice in the trash," she says. "It was over half-full and had been wiped down."

"So the killer probably purchased an identical carton of juice, poured some out to match how much was left in Andrew's and laced it with the antifreeze, wiping down the other one and throwing it away."

"That would be my guess," she says.

"So the killer had to know what kind of juice he drank and have access to his kitchen," I say. "It wouldn't take him long to make the switch, but it'd take a few minutes —especially to sneak the other carton out and throw it away."

"If they had a key he wouldn't even have had to have been there for them to do it," she says.

"Was there a hide-a-key found outside?"

She shakes her head and takes another bite and a sip of her tea.

"So either there was and the killer kept it," I say, "or he or she has a key of their own, or he broke in, or did it while Andrew was there. Was any antifreeze found in the house or the shed or in his vehicle?"

"No. Not a trace. Were you thinking maybe it was self-inflicted?"

"Not really, but I wanted to rule it out. And to see if—"

"It looks like the can with the cross cut out in it we found in the dumpster at Ace is the source. We'll have to wait for lab results to be sure, but I'm being told it's pretty likely."

I nod and neither of us says anything while we eat some more.

"You just need to find out if anyone bought him orange juice recently," she says.

"Yes, I do," I say. "And I know who I'm going to ask first."

26

"Did anyone grocery shop for Andrew?" I ask.

"Not really," Peggy Munn says.

I'm back in the car after lunch, speaking to Peggy by phone as I head to Ace because Dawn texted to let me know she may have found out something that might help my investigation.

"I'd pick up a few things for him from time to time," Peggy is saying, her voice sounding more like that of an old lady on the phone than it did when I spoke with her person. "Especially if I thought he wasn't eating like he should."

She may not have been his girlfriend but she certainly acted like it. Whether they were lovers as so many suspected or just the platonic friends she claims, she took better care of him than most people ever get.

"How often was that?" I ask.

"Not very. Maybe once every week or so. Well, wait now . . . you know . . . now that I think about it . . . I probably picked up a few things for him every time I was doing my grocery shopping, but . . . it wasn't like I was doing his shopping. I was . . . I guess I was just sort of supplementing what he did. That's why it didn't really occur to me. I definitely didn't do his shopping. But I guess I got him stuff pretty regularly."

"Can you think of what the last few things you got for him were?"

"Well, now, let me see. No, not really. My mind's not what it used to be. I can give it a think and see what I come up with though. Could also pull out my receipt and see if it might jog my— Something I bought him didn't kill him, did it? Please tell me no. Did he die of some kind of food poisoning or something? Oh, my mercy, please don't let it be something I gave him."

"I'm sure it wasn't," I say. "This is related to something else."

"Oh good. Thank you, God. I wouldn't be able to live with myself if something I did led to his—"

"Would you mind checking your receipt for me?"

"Not at all," she says. "Can I call you back once I've located it?"

"Sure."

"Oh, you know . . . I'm pretty sure Andrew said that

his neighbor Maddy Smith brought him some food recently. Really surprised him. Me too, come to that. Said it was like she felt guilty for something and was trying to make up for it. Said she did it when her husband wasn't home and kept looking over her shoulder for him to pull up the whole time she was standing at his door. Oh, and I think that foulmouthed little girl whose dad donated the land the church is on—what's her name? Ah—"

"Melissa?"

"Yeah, Melissa Epps. Such a pretty little girl to have such a potty mouth on her. Always makes me think of that song—you know, the one by the Allman Brothers."

"'Sweet Melissa,'" I say.

"Yeah. Always found it ironic that hearing her name made me think of it, 'cause that child is anything but sweet. She's mean Melissa."

"Did Andrew talk about her a lot?"

"A fair amount I guess, now that I think of it," she says. "I think he had a sweet spot for her. 'Course he was just one big sweet spot really. I think he felt bad for her and was trying to help her. Anyway . . . She used to come over sometimes. She reads a lot and you know how well read Andrew was. They had a sort of unofficial book club—just the two of them. She'd ask him questions about whatever she was reading. He'd read all the classics and could talk to her about all of them. Anyway, I think when she snuck over she'd bring snacks sometimes. Andrew thought it was sweet. I think maybe she had a bit of a crush—not physically, but to the kindness of his soul and the prowess of his mind. I don't know. Anyway . . . I can't think of anyone else. Except. Wait. Maybe . . . Seems like one of the workers at Ace would bring him some things from time to time. I think maybe it was stuff his girlfriend made, though sometimes it was just like a bag of groceries. Andrew said he thought the young man was working up his nerve to talk to him about something or maybe to confess something. But in typical Andrew fashion he didn't push him. He was just waiting for the boy to work up his nerve. I don't know. I could be wrong about all that. That's just what came to mind when you asked about anyone getting him groceries."

"Any idea who it was?" I ask. "What his name is?"

"No, sorry, but . . . wait a minute. No, it's . . . I just don't know. I do remember that it was a name from the Bible I think."

"Like the name of a book of the Bible or just a name that's in the Bible?"

"I'm not sure, but I think it was just in the Bible not the name of a book. But I could be wrong. Probably am."

"That's helpful," I say. "Thanks. Just call me when you find the receipt."

"Will do, sweetie. Sure thing. Just as soon as I do."

I end the call as I'm pulling into the Ace parking lot

from Highway 71, and before I have even parked another call comes in.

Seeing that it's Reggie, I answer it right away.

"Whatta you doin?" she asks.

I tell her.

"Got time to go over everything with me when you finish there?"

"Sure."

"I just sent you the recording of the 911 call. Give it a listen before you call so we can talk about it too."

"Ten-four."

"Talk to you then. Will be our last time to go over it before everything becomes about the storm."

Finding a parking spot a little ways down so that I'm not directly in front of the building, I shut off the engine and open my phone to listen to the 911 call. It takes a few moments to download and while it does I connect my phone to the car's sound system so I can play it through the speakers.

911, what's your emergency?

Somebody's dead.

Who? What is the address?

The ex-priest in Wewa . . . He's dead. Been killed.

What's your address? Are you with him?

702

(Background) can . . . use forklift.

702 what?

No. Not—that was wrong. 788 North Highway 71.

(Background) We have a customer (inaudible) for treated two-by-fours.

Who am I speaking with?

You want his name?

What is your name?

Andrew Irwin.

Are you with the victim now, Andrew?

I'm not Andrew. He is.

The victim's name is Andrew? Can you wait with him until emergency services arrive?

No.

(Background) Loud truck engine. Maybe a child squealing. Maybe a dog barking in the distance. A horn beeping. A loud wooden crack like a bat hitting something maybe. Two men laughing loudly.

What is your name? Where are you?

(Inaudible)

(Background) Where you at? Need . . . help . . . sending him out. Hey big fella.

Hey, please don't do that. Please leave her alone, okay?

Please leave who alone? Are you okay? What is your name? Where are you? Sounds like a lot is going on there?

I'm not going to tell you any of that. Andrew is dead. Goodbye.

27

"I didn't realize it earlier or I would've mentioned it," Dawn is saying. "And it may mean nothing. Probably does. But . . . Levi Tucker showed up for work late yesterday."

When I stepped into the store, Dawn met me and asked me to step back out front with her for a moment. We are now standing on the left side of the front porch near several extension ladders, a cable running through them and attached to the building for security.

"He's the one who walked Father Andrew back home the day before," she says. "And went back to check on him later that day."

"How often does he show up late?"

"Never," she says. "Literally, that was the first time."

I nod as I consider it.

Most of the customers going in and out of the store speak or wave to us as they do. Several of them greet both of us by name, and I realize again just how much this town has become home to me, and just how quickly it has happened.

"I worked in daycare for twenty years," Dawn says. "Between retiring from that and starting here, I subbed at the high school for a while. Built up a rapport with some of the kids. Levi's girlfriend, Auburn McLemore, was one of them."

"Okay," I say, not quite sure where she's going.

"She drove Levi to work yesterday," she says. "Also a first."

"Think she'll talk to me?" I ask.

She nods. "She's waiting for you in my office right now. She says she's scared of him, so I've sent him on a delivery to Mexico Beach, so he'll be a while, but we've got to make sure we have her out of here before he gets back."

I shake my head in wonder. "You're . . . Thank you very much. And if you ever decide you want to leave hardware . . . we could use you at the sheriff's department."

As if believing her name requires it, Auburn McLemore's hair is dyed a deep auburn that reminds me of Jann Arden's hair back during her *Living Under June* days.

She is small, pale, and frail with green, cat-like eyes that avoid all but the most minimal contact.

Dawn is in here with us and her office door is closed.

"You don't have to tell us anything you don't want to," Dawn says. "But anything you do tell us we'll keep a secret. Levi will never know. You have our word on that."

Auburn glances at me and I nod.

"I've sent Levi on a delivery to Mexico Beach and I told him to call me before he leaves there because I might need him to pick something up for me, so you're safe. He'll never know you were here."

"K," Auburn says in a low, quiet voice, so soft it's barely audible.

"Do you want to tell Detective Jordan some of the things you've told me?"

Auburn shrugs. "I guess." She glances at me, then looks down, though still in my direction. "He . . . Levi is . . . He hits me. Does . . . other stuff too. Makes me do stuff I don't want to. But . . . he says if I ever try to leave him he'll kill me and . . . I know he means it. I know he would."

What was it Margaret Atwood said? Men are afraid women will laugh at them. Women are afraid men will kill them.

Dawn says, "Is that the only reason you're still with him?"

She nods. "Yes, ma'am."

"Well, whenever you decide to leave him, I'm sure John here can arrange protection for you."

That's something that's not nearly as easy as most people think. And it requires the complete cooperation of the battered woman, which we often don't get.

"If you are serious about leaving him and can really commit to never contacting him again and doing everything we tell you to do," I say, "we can get you a place in a shelter. But just know that your life will change radically. You'll be saying goodbye to everything for a while. I hope you will. I hope you are willing to do whatever it takes to get your life back, but for it to work you have to be one-hundred percent certain and totally and completely committed."

"Are you?" Dawn asks her.

She shakes her head. "Not yet."

"Well, I hope you will be soon," Dawn says.

"Thank you."

"You can get in touch with me anytime," I say. "I'll help you in any way I can."

She gives a slight nod without really looking up at me.

"Can you tell us about yesterday morning?" Dawn says.

"I was asleep at my house," she says. "He calls me and tells me to get my lazy ass up, he needs a ride to work. I started to ask him what was wrong with his truck but he told me not to ask any lame-ass questions, to just shut the fuck up and come get him. So I did. But . . . he was only a little ways away from work anyway. But he was walking in the opposite direction. He was almost to Blue Gator. About half a mile from the old Catholic church. He acted all wired and shit, like he was on something, but he wouldn't tell me where he had been or what he had been doing or why he wanted me to pick him up when he was so close to work as it was. Or why he was walking in the wrong direction."

"Do you have any idea what he was doing or where his vehicle was?" I ask.

She shakes her head. "No, sir. None. I really can't imagine."

"Did he ever mention Father Andrew?" I ask.

She shrugs. "Not really. Couple of times he had some vegetables from his garden I think. He's always talkin' about teaching people lessons, showing them the truth. Think maybe it was about the old priest a few times, but not sure."

"Okay," I say. "Thank you. Now, let's get you out of here. And remember what I said . . . If you ever do decide to end it with Levi and are serious about having a different life and never going back to him, call me. It will be the hardest thing you ever do, but it will be worth it and it's your best hope for a good life."

. . .

"YOU DIDN'T SEEM TOO encouraging of Auburn leaving Levi," Dawn says after Auburn is gone.

"I hope I didn't come across as discouraging," I say, "but . . . it's—it'll be the most difficult thing she's ever done by far. She has to want it—I mean more than anything. It can't be something she's talked into or that she kinda sorta wants maybe. I want a far, far better life for her, but the only hope of her ever having that is if she chooses it. We can help her . . . *a lot*—but only *after* she commits. Not before. She's got to do it."

"I hope she will," she says.

"I do too."

"But?"

"But, unfortunately, tragically, chances are slim. Extremely slim. And it's also dangerous. Roughly seventy-five percent of battered women killed by their abuser were killed while confronting them or trying to escape."

28

"Sounds like you're making really good progress on the case," Reggie is saying. "Shame it's about to come to a screeching halt."

"Yes, it is," I say.

Because of the approach of Hurricane Michael, all investigations are being suspended so that everyone in the sheriff's department can assist with the more pressing issues related to the storm and its aftermath.

Hurricane Michael continues to grow and intensify. TV weather maps of the Gulf are filled with a massive, monstrous, swirling red mass of chaos and destruction inching its way toward the textured green drawing depicting Florida.

I'm driving home to help Anna pack and get things

ready for the storm. I've just given Reggie an update on the case.

"I know you'll continue to work on it mentally," she says, "and hopefully we'll get lucky and you can get back on it in a day or two, but . . . it's looking like this could wind up being the big one—maybe even our Katrina."

Hurricanes are usually slow moving and unpredictable but the closer they get the better idea we have about just how hard a shot to the mouth we're going to get. The storm still has nearly seventeen hours over the warm waters of the Gulf to intensify, so we could be looking at a violent, brutal, knockout punch, depending on where we are in relation to the swing. We just won't know until the punch actually lands.

To best be prepared to assist the citizens of our county after the storm, our department is going to twelve hour shifts and we're stationing our people in different regions of the county. That way if an area gets cut off from the others we'll have personnel there to help keep order and provide security and assistance.

"And I hate it for the little McLemore girl," she adds. "Hurricanes increase domestic violence like a mofo."

"Should I have intervened more?" I ask.

I think about how my *intervening* in a recent school shooting case cost a boy his life, and wonder if the guilt and shame and pain of that experience has me more reticent to take action these days.

"No, you're right," she says. "Until she's ready . . . all you'd be doing is making her life more dangerous."

"I wonder . . ."

"Don't start second-guessing yourself," she says. "It'll drive you crazy."

"I'm not just starting," I say. "I'm an old pro at it."

"Do you have a sense of who committed the murder yet?" she asks. "I know you haven't had time to build a case yet. I just wondered if you've already got a prime suspect or actually know who did it even if you can't prove it yet."

"No," I say. "Not really. A few of the possible suspects are stronger than others, but I've yet to uncover a motive. So, no. I've got nothing—apart from a little information and a ton of questions."

"You buying what everybody's saying about Andrew?" she says.

"That he was a good, decent man not mixed up in anything that would get him killed? Yeah. I do. I knew him. Worked with him for several years as a prison volunteer. All they're doing is confirming what I already knew about him. And the fact that it's so unanimous. Everyone is saying the same thing about him—regardless of how little or well they knew him. That's because it's his character, who he was."

"Gonna make it a lot harder to make a case," she says.

"Let alone be able to prove it. Low risk victims are the worst."

Certain circumstances and behaviors cause a person to be at greater risk of having a crime committed against them than others. Someone who lives in a high crime area is far more likely to become a victim than someone who doesn't. Someone who is involved in criminal activities or frequents places where crime is committed is far more likely to become a victim of a crime. Someone like Father Andrew is about as least likely to be a victim as one can get. The safe small-town environment, his solitary existence, his age and occupation, and his lifestyle all put him at a very low risk of being murdered, which makes solving his murder all the more challenging.

For me, looking at a victim's risk levels is not about blaming the victim for what befell them but trying to determine where and how and when and why the paths of predator and prey intersected.

"Yes it is," I say. "Add to that having to pause the investigation for the storm . . ."

"I hate to say it—" she says.

"Then don't," I say. "If you're going to say anything about it going unsolved."

"How many unsolveds you got?" she asks.

"Way too many," I say.

"They follow you around, don't they?" she says. "Haunting you like unquiet spirits."

"This one isn't going to end that way," I say.

"Hope not."

"It's not," I say. "It won't. I won't let it."

"Oh, so you let those others go unsolved?"

"They're still open as far as I'm concerned," I say. "I still pull out the files and work them when I can."

"Oh, so there's no such thing as unsolveds," she says. "Just not solved yet."

29

"What kind of cases are the most difficult to solve?" Anna asks.

"Motiveless ones," I say. "Or, well, ones where the motive is only known to the killer and has little or nothing to do with the victim."

We are in the kitchen packing up food and medicine for her and the girls to take to her parents' when they evacuate, the latest coverage of Hurricane Michael playing softly on the TV in the living room. Johanna and Taylor are in their beds fast asleep, only vaguely aware they'll be evacuating in the morning and why.

"Exactly," she says.

"So you're saying Reggie's right," I say.

"I'm *saying* that's what this one sounds like."

I nod. She's right. That's exactly what it is. Which is

why Reggie's comments bothered me so much. The thought of failing to solve Andrew's murder is something I can't even consider.

"I know," I say. "I just don't want it to be."

"And when has that ever changed anything?"

I smile. "Never."

I well know that accepting what is instead of wishing for what I want to be is the way not only to peace but to doing my best work—but right now I really don't want to be reminded of that.

On the TV two male meteorologists are talking about what Michael is doing now and what he's likely to do. "Sustained winds of 120 miles per hour so far, but it's strengthening. What we're seeing right here on these satellite images is intensification. Just how much intensification we don't know, but . . . Will it reach 150 miles per hour by landfall? More? We just don't know. But it's not out of the question. And if it does . . . well, folks, that is going to be . . . catastrophic, just catastrophic. At this moment Michael is approximately 249 miles out from Panama City, Florida. Expect gale force winds beginning overnight and landfall to occur between one and four in the afternoon. This is an extremely dangerous storm. And it is likely to be devastating."

"Oh my God," Anna says. I turn to see her standing beside me staring at the TV.

"The pressure is dropping rapidly," one of the meteorologists is saying. "The winds haven't caught up with it yet, but when they do . . ."

Ordinarily an underreactor to hurricanes, I have been unusually wary of this one. Until now I had thought that I may have been thinking the storm was going to be worse than what it will actually be because of the dream I had, but it may be even worse than I have feared.

"I really wish you were going with us," she says.

"I'm gonna feel a lot better when y'all are safe and sound in Dothan," I say.

"Yeah, but how am I gonna feel being up there with you down here?"

"Sure you don't want to go ahead and go tonight?" I say.

"I can't," she says. "Still have too much to do—work and getting the house ready. I thought about seeing if I could get Carla to help me in the morning before we leave. Maybe even talk her and John Paul into going with us. But I don't know. Rudy was there again this evening when I picked the girls up."

We had offered for Carla and John Paul to stay here with us when we thought we'd be here and then to go with Anna and the girls when we decided they were going to her parents' place in Dothan, but both times she declined, saying she was going to her dad's place in Pottersville so she could help him during the storm.

"I wish she would," I say. "And as far as the house, we'll get as much done tonight as we can and then you can leave the rest for me."

"But when you leave in the morning you won't be back here until . . . who knows when, but definitely after the hurricane hits."

"I might be able to get Jake or Merrill to help," I say. "Just want y'all to leave as early as possible. There will probably be a lot of evacuation traffic."

We still need to move the patio furniture into the garage," she says. "And strap down the trash can. Are we going to tape the windows? We really need to put the rest of our pictures and important papers in those plastic storage crates and take them upstairs."

Anna's Mustang is too small to be able to transport her and the girls and all their clothes and supplies *and* the crates of our pictures and important papers.

One of the things we've done to mitigate any possible loss we may incur is to snap digital pictures of our pictures with our phones, so we'll at least have backups that we can have printed one day if need be.

"Flooding's not going to be an issue for us here," I say. "Wind and falling trees will be far more likely to get our house."

"We'll get flooding if the roof is blown off or the windows are shattered," she says.

Our home was built in 1968 and we have been repairing and remodeling as we can. We've replaced a lot of the old thin, single-paned windows with much better, thicker, insulated, weatherproof windows, but not all of them, and it's hard to imagine the old, thin 1968 windows withstanding sustained winds of 150 miles per hour or more and gusts up to 200.

"From rain coming in, yeah. I meant we won't have any storm surge this far in," I say. "We won't have flooding as in water rolling in on the ground floor. My point was I think the crates of pictures would be safer downstairs—in the middle of the house, like the hall closet."

"Oh," she says. "Okay. You're probably right."

"And when it comes to these storms," one of the meteorologists is saying, "the pressure is the thing. Pay attention to the pressure."

"Yes," the other one says. "And you can tell from this satellite imagery . . . I mean . . . look at it. It's just ominous. *Ominous.* This is even more concerning than it was originally. It is intensifying very quickly. I can't overemphasize it enough. This is getting very very very serious very very quickly. Storm surge for Mexico Beach is projected for up to 13 feet but that's going to go up, I can guarantee that."

"Should we turn it off?" Anna asks.

Before I can respond she is pointing the remote toward the screen and pressing the power button.

"Sure I can't talk you into quitting and coming with us?" she says.

I laugh.

"I'm only half kidding," she says. "You can always find another job. I can't find another you."

30

The next morning, with the hurricane just a few hours from landfall, I'm on my way to the sheriff's department.

The sky already has that distinctive, odd amber glow that signals the approach of an existential storm of apocalyptic proportions.

Carla has the girls and Anna is finishing up a few preparations, packing, then going to pick up Verna, my dad's wife, who late last night decided to evacuate with Anna and the girls to Anna's parents'. Dad, unwilling to leave, is going to remain behind to take care of their place and help out with emergency services after the storm passes.

I'm running later than I intended after helping with

the packing and house prep, but it's really only for the aftermath of the storm that I'll be needed.

I've made it as far as Honeyville when I get the call.

"That stolen van you saw at Ace," Reggie says. "With the sketchy guys with the stolen credit card in it."

"Yeah?"

"We found it," she says. "It's been torched and there's a body in it. Can you go straight there?"

Ten minutes later I'm pulling up to a dilapidated old barn on the backside of a hayfield in Dalkeith, the wind already picking up, the rain coming down in intermittent spits.

The flat fields on either side of the narrow dirt road leading back to the barn are dotted with large round rolls of hay that have recently been harvested.

What little paint there is left on the barn is a red so dark it's almost crimson.

Parking beside the patrol car at the end of the road, the only other vehicle visible, I kill the engine and climb out.

The moment I get out of the car I can smell the char and smoke, the acrid odor of an electrical fire and the sweet savory aroma of cooked meat.

I walk around to the back of the barn to find Deputy Tony Harris staring at the scorched van, his nose pinched between the thumb and forefinger of his left hand.

"Can't imagine I'll be able to eat barbecue anytime soon," he says. "Or ever again."

The vehicle is white and looks to be a late 90s Chevy Astro cargo van. All the glass is broken out, the tires are melted, and there are black smoke and char marks in the faded white paint around the windows.

The back doors are both open as wide as they'll go and inside in the pugilist position is a human body—too badly burned to be able to determine age, sex, race, or virtually anything else.

"Takes a lot of intense heat and time to burn a vehicle and a body this bad," I say.

I think about the Phoenix, an inmate I worked with at Potter Correctional Institution who burned his victims after he was finished raping and torturing them, and a case that Sam Michaels and Daniel Davis worked where the killer actually used fire as his weapon, making burnt offerings of the sacrifices his sick psyche demanded.

"They'd've had all the time they needed," he says. "Way back here away from the road, woods on all sides. No neighbors."

"Anonymous tip," he says.

"Anonymous tip?" I say. "What does that mean?"

"Means I got a cousin who's dickin' a married woman on the side," he says. "They came back here this morning to have one final roll in the hay so to speak before the hurricane blows us all away. Saw it and called me. *Anonymously.*"

"Oh," I say, "an *anonymous* tip."

"Yeah."

"I'll keep him out of it if I can," I say, "and either way we won't involve the woman—unless that's her husband in there—but I'll need to talk to him."

"Sure. No problem."

A horn sounds from the front side of the barn and I walk around to see who it is while Tony continues to watch the van.

I find Jessica Young, our department's forensics specialist, getting out of our crime scene unit van.

"You mind helping me carry my stuff around there?" she says.

"Not at all," I say, "but you can probably pull a little closer."

"This is fine. I don't have much and I want to preserve any prints or vehicle tracks."

I nod.

"You probably already guessed this," she says, "but FDLE isn't going to send their people over with the storm on its way. ME's office neither. I'll photograph and measure and document everything as best I can but I seriously doubt we can get a tow truck out here to move the van before the storm hits and I have no idea what to do with the body."

"I'll see what I can do about moving the van and body while you're working the scene," I say.

Half an hour later, after helping Jessica set up her equipment, I am back around in front of the barn making calls, asking for favors, coming up empty.

As I see it we have three options. Leave the van here until after the storm, tow it somewhere in the area to store it during the storm, though no obvious place comes to mind except for maybe the school's bus barn, or leave it here but post a deputy to watch it—something that seems an unnecessary risk given the size and power of the storm about to land on top of us.

As I'm tapping in Reggie's number to ask her what I should do, I get a call from Carla.

She's hysterical.

"Oh, God, John, I'm so sorry. I'm so . . . I fucked up. I—"

"What is it?" I ask. "Calm down and tell me what's going on."

"I fell asleep," she says.

My heart starts racing.

"I—I didn't sleep much last night," she says. "John Paul was up a lot and I was worried about the hurricane. I was actually dozing off this morning as I was watching the kids. Oh fuck. Oh God. I'm so—"

"What is it, Carla?" I ask. "Tell me what happened."

"I tried to call Anna but she's not answering."

"Okay. Just tell me. What is it? What happened?"

"I couldn't stay awake. I tried but I just couldn't."

"Has something happened to one of the kids?"

"Dad came by and could see how sleepy I was. He told me to take a little nap. He'd watch the three of them for me while I got a little rest."

"Okay."

"I fell asleep hard," she says. "I must have . . . I just woke up. John, he's gone with them. He left me a note saying not to worry. He'll take good care of them. That he's worried about his brother and that he was going to get him to evacuate him to Pottersville with us and that he'd be back soon, but . . . John, his brother lives in Mexico Beach. They're driving straight toward the storm . . . and even if nothing goes wrong I don't think they can be back before it hits."

31

I'm speeding down 71 toward Overstreet, my emergency lights flashing, my mind racing much faster than my car.

The outer bands of the storm have come ashore—the pavement is damp and slick, the air is warm and muggy, raindrops gently falling, lightly splatting on my windshield.

Though Port St. Joe and Mexico Beach are under a mandatory evacuation, some residents will inevitably disregard it, others wait until it's nearly too late. The latter group causes traffic on 71 to be heavy, and it makes me wish my car was equipped with a siren and not just the small emergency lights behind my grille.

Weaving in and out of the line of evacuees, using my horn as a siren, spending as much time as possible in the empty left lane, I call Reggie as I pass through Honeyville.

"Oh my God, John," she says. "Of course, do what you've got to do. I'll call Tony and Jessica and tell them what to do with the van and the body. Don't worry about that."

I'm not. I'm not worried about anything but finding my children and getting them to safety. But it goes without saying so I don't voice what she's got to already know.

"Do we have anyone on Overstreet?" I ask. "Who's in Mexico Beach?"

"We've got Padgett at the fire station and—"

"Can you have them look for Rudy's old red Cadillac?" I ask. "But make sure they don't chase him. Chances are this early he's already—"

"I'll let them know," she says. "But it's already coming in over there so I'm not sure what all they'll be able to do. But I'll tell them. John, just be careful. Latest reports are it's going to be at least a four—maybe even a five. We've never seen anything like this before. I know you're not going to stop until you find them, but just remember you can't find them if something happens to you."

"He doesn't even have them in car seats," I say. "They'd be in danger even if he wasn't driving them straight into a superstorm. I . . . I just . . ."

I am unable to say anything else for a moment.

"Okay," she says. "It's going to be okay. Let me call everyone down there and let them know what's going on. I'll get them on it right away. You just be careful, John. I'll call you back in a few."

When I turn onto Overstreet, the road that in approximately twenty miles dead-ends into the Gulf of Mexico and Michael, I find the right lane completely empty and I gun the engine as both the rain and the wind increase.

There are a few last-minute evacuees in the left lane, but not many, and I scan each one carefully, not just looking for Rudy's car but for him and the girls in case his car broke down and they caught a ride back with someone else.

The rain makes it difficult to see but I'm fairly certain they've not been in any of the vehicles I've passed so far.

After a few houses clumped close to 71, Overstreet becomes an empty desolate highway lined by planted pinewood forests, broken up occasionally by the fenced-in fields of farms, hardwood hammocks, or the cypress-ringed fringes of wetlands. Primarily a connector road between Highway 71 in Wewa and Highway 98 in Mexico Beach, the mostly empty Overstreet gets its name because it rises above the Intracoastal Waterway.

My phone begins vibrating and I lift it out of the seat to see that Anna is calling.

"Carla just called me," she says. "Have you found them?"

"Not yet," I say. "I'm on Overstreet now, but just a few miles down it."

"I can't believe that bastard has our kids in his old piece of shit car driving into a— Oh, John, I'm really sacred."

"Me too," I say.

"Just being with him is dangerous," she says, "but actually driving into a hurricane . . . What the hell was he thinking?"

"His brain is pickled," I say. "So there's no telling. But he's probably genuinely concerned about his brother, who he adores. Probably thought he was doing Carla a favor by letting her sleep, and . . . I can't help but think that . . . maybe he thought that by taking them he'd be assured that we'd come get them, help him and his brother, if anything happened."

"Like they're his goddamn insurance?" she says.

"Maybe."

"I can't ever remember being this angry," she says. "Of course, I'm sure I was at Chris at some point. I think if I saw Rudy right now I'd kill him with my bare hands. How can I help? What can I do? I'm just coming back into town with Verna now. Should I head your way?"

"Just go to our house and get things ready. I'll try to get them and get back there as quickly as I can, but best-case scenario we'll have to ride out the storm there."

"But—"

The call drops and when I try to call her again I see that I have no cell service, which makes me think at least one of the towers has already been blown down.

Dropping the phone onto the seat, I turn up my wipers to the fastest speed and I stomp on the gas to go even faster, feeling the backend of the car fishtail a little on the wet asphalt.

32

The tall pines lining the rural highway are being blown about like saplings, whipping back and forth some, but mostly just bending, their tops all tilting in the same direction—which I assume is toward the center of the storm's swirl.

The wet road before me is empty, flat, and straight, its vanishing point stretching toward an ominous horizon.

With no phone and no passengers to talk to, I begin to pray and contemplate, attempting to calm my racing heart and noisy mind with mindful breathing.

I pray for protection and safety for my girls and for little John Paul, innocents all, dependent on us to take care of them—something we failed to do at this most critical of times.

I pray for our area and for all those about to feel the ferocious, pitiless power of Michael.

After a few moments I check my phone again. Still no cell service, which is further indication there isn't going to be until after the storm—and perhaps well beyond.

My rage at Rudy comes in waves, rising out of the hot lava core of my being, emanating out of my father's heart with a vitriolic energy that causes me to shake.

What I feel for Carla is less intense and more frustration and exasperation than anger.

I also feel guilty. I should have figured out a way to help Anna more, to finish things last night or keep the girls this morning or just insist that they leave yesterday.

To try to calm down again and to keep my mind from going completely mad with worry, I begin to review Andrew's murder and apply myself to figuring out who killed him.

No matter how much I think about it, I'm having a difficult time identifying a credible motive. Of course, motives are often incredible or even nonexistent.

It's possible Father Andrew was killed by a stranger. It's just not as likely as someone he knew.

Of the people known to him I don't really even have a prime suspect yet. Levi has lied to me. He's abusive and violent and he has a connection to Ace where the call was made and the murder weapon was found. But beyond that thin circumstantial evidence there is nothing that points to him being the killer. There could be. It's possible I just haven't turned it up yet.

And the truth is, Levi is no more connected to Andrew than Dawn is. Do I not suspect her because she's been so helpful? Has she been so helpful so I won't suspect her? It's possible she's actually setting Levi up. She's the one who had him take Andrew home and go back and check on him.

Of course Tad Yon and Maddy Smith could have killed him in some misguided attempt to protect their sons from a threat that didn't exist. Perhaps Maddy didn't just take Andrew food. Maybe she took him drink too.

Or maybe it was Little Ben Trainer getting revenge for the death of his dog. People have certainly killed for a lot less. Or maybe it was his meth mom, Marie Ann. She could've have stolen something we don't yet know about or maybe just did it because something in her meth mind told her to.

Peggy Munn or her husband are good possibilities also. I only have Peggy's word that Andrew felt the same for her as she did for him. Maybe he rejected her and she killed him for it. Or maybe her husband killed him out of jealousy and trying to get his wife back.

Or maybe it was Jan Epps, no longer able to tolerate the injustice and sacrilege of not only not having her land revert back to her but having a priest she disdains defile what once was a sacred place to her. Or maybe it was her troubled stepdaughter who lied to me about how well she knew Andrew and how much interaction she had with him.

Of course, it could be none of these. It could be someone else entirely—maybe even someone I haven't even encountered yet.

As much as I try to focus on Andrew's case and the questions I have about it, all I can really think about is the fact that my girls are out here in this dangerous storm with a drunk driver and no car seat.

They're going to die, a voice in my head says.

"No," I say out loud. "No they are not."

Who's going to stop it from happening? You?

Because of the storm, because of how helpless and powerless I feel, lines from the book of Job swirl around in my head.

Then the Lord answered Job out of the whirlwind, and said,

Who is this that darkeneth counsel by words without knowledge?

Gird up now thy loins like a man; for I will demand of thee, and answer thou me.

Where wast thou when I laid the foundations of the earth? declare, if thou hast understanding.

Who hath laid the measures thereof, if thou knowest? or who hath stretched the line upon it?

Whereupon are the foundations thereof fastened? or who laid the corner stone thereof;

When the morning stars sang together, and all the sons of God shouted for joy?

Or who shut up the sea with doors, when it broke forth, as if it had issued out of the womb?

When I made the cloud the garment thereof, and thick darkness a swaddling band for it,

And broke up for it my decreed place, and set bars and doors,

And said, Hitherto shalt thou come, but no further: and here shall thy proud waves be stayed?

Hath the rain a father? or who hath begotten the drops of dew?

Out of whose womb came the ice? and the hoary frost of heaven, who hath gendered it?

Canst thou draw out Leviathan with an hook? or his tongue with a cord which thou lettest down?

Canst thou put an hook into his nose? or bore his jaw through with a thorn?

I'm racing to save my children from Leviathan and don't have so much as a hook.

33

The empty, bleak road seems to stretch on forever and it feels like even at nearly 90 miles per hour I'm not getting anywhere.

More of Michael is ashore now, but just the outer edges. I suspect this is merely an approved-for-all-audiences preview of coming attractions.

The rain has increased and, driven by the wind, turned into a barrage of bullet-like drops that pelt the vehicle with a velocity I wouldn't have thought possible before now.

The wind has intensified too. Its sustained force bending the tall narrow pines to over a 45-degree angle, pressing them to just before the point of breaking. Its gusts actually shifting my car about on the highway.

I'm almost certain I'm still in the outer bands, and I've never seen anything quite like this.

The slanting sheets of rain make it difficult to see, the frenetically swiping wipers impotent against the deluge.

The whirring of the wind is haunting and ominous, something about its whistling, silent sound making me feel even more isolated and lonely.

The asphalt highway is so wet and slick, the wind so fierce and powerful, the driving, windswept rain so thick and impenetrable, I know I should slow down and drive more cautiously but I can't. I just can't do anything but race toward my children as fast as I can.

I realize when I think of rescuing my children I am thinking of all three—my two girls and the baby boy who for far too short a time was my son.

When I round the next curve, I turn into heavier rain and more intense winds.

The highway is littered with limbs and leaves and debris, all clinging wetly to the asphalt.

The quality of light in the sky has changed. The day is darker now, more monochromatic, its gray different in tone and texture than the more ordinary overcast iterations.

As I continue, the debris on the road increases, larger limbs and branches beginning to block sections of the road.

Visibility drops even further. It's like I'm trying to see

underwater, except for the briefest of moments when the wipers first cut a swath through the pool of rain and before it refills the spot.

I'm forced to slow down and to drive in a more zigzag pattern.

But even attempting to navigate around the larger clumps of tree and debris I'm still bouncing over plenty that I shouldn't be, my car thudding hard back onto the pavement after catching air and having its tires spin freely for a moment, its backend fishtailing and causing me to swerve when the rubber of the rear tires makes contact with the wet asphalt again.

Even as I'm trying desperately to avoid debris and keep my car on the road, I'm searching for Rudy's car, scanning the ditches and side roads for any sign of the kidnapper I intend to arrest and file charges against. But there is no sign of him or anyone else.

I'm in a dark, wet world, completely abandoned by all others.

My head fills and my ears pop as the pressure continues to drop.

As the ferocious wind continues to intensify, the leaning pines are forced even farther down—some to the breaking point.

The crack and splinter of twenty-year-old, thick-bodied pines as if they're little saplings is followed by the creaks and grains of them falling and the soft, brushy thud of them hitting the wet ground a few moments later.

Given the wind and the rain and wipers, the snap and moan and eventual earthy impact of the falling trees sounds like it's happening a great distance away, as if I'm in a deep wood hearing an unseen tree within the remote range fall.

With every mile I travel, the storm seems to intensify exponentially, and I wonder just how scared Johanna, Taylor, and John Paul are.

If they're still alive, the same hateful voice in my head from before says.

"They are," I say. "And I'm going to find them."

Unlike previous trips down here, I don't see the Overstreet Bridge until I am right up on it. Usually, it can be seen looming in the distance for a few miles before it is reached—it and the forestry division fire tower to the left of it rising some 100 feet into the air.

I glance to my left as I begin to ascend the bridge and see that the steel frame structure of the tower is being blown about, swaying and twisting in the violent wind.

Driving up the bridge that rises high into the air and extends quite a distance to the other side of the Intracoastal, I feel even more vulnerable, my route even more treacherous. The wind is more forceful and my tires have more trouble finding traction on the wet inclining pavement.

I hear glass shattering and turn to see the the fire tower's lookout post windows raining down onto the steel as the wooden enclosure breaks apart and begins to fly away, shingles and wood and metal and glass being lifted into the air and flung about.

A moment later, with a loud metallic creak and groan the entire tower falls, its 100-foot-tall ladder-like frame clanging loudly onto the soggy limb-and-leaves-covered earth below.

It is in this moment, watching the steel tower that had been through so many other storms bend and twist and fall, that I realize just how different and devastating Michael is going to be, and I wonder what chance I really have of finding Taylor, Johanna, and John Paul alive.

34

Feeling like I'm the last man on a dangerous and hostile planet, I continue on.

I'm having to go far more slowly now than I would like—down the bridge, around and over debris, straining to see the road through the wind-driven rain being hurled at my car.

My ears continue to pop and my head continues to hurt from the drop in barometric pressure.

The few houses around the bridge are dark and abandoned. The only lights I can see anywhere come from the headlights of my car, and they are mostly absorbed in the wet gray wall I'm perpetually moving headlong into.

The shaking, twisting pines continue to snap and fall, their bark splintering and breaking open about a quarter of the way up, the light golden wood inside cracking and fracturing, appearing like mangled bone showing through splitting skin.

Power lines bounce about like a child's jump rope, holding the upper half of snapped-in-two light poles as they dangle like small limbs caught in Spanish moss.

For a while blowing transformers emit loud bangs and an arc of glowing blue flame into the storm's cacophony and the day's wet grayness, but eventually no sound or light comes from them.

The road continues to be littered with increasing amounts of debris. Joining the branches and leaves are the tops of trees, downed power poles, and jangling electrical lines, and I wonder how long it will be until I reach debris that I can neither drive around nor ride over.

Coming up in a mile or so I have a decision to make.

According to Carla, Rudy's brother, Carl, lives near the marina. Up ahead there's a residential road that veers off to the right to come out farther west down 98 closer to the marina. Do I turn on it, assuming that Rudy would take the obvious shortcut or do I stay straight and dead-end into 98 next to the Lookout and take the more scenic route along the Gulf through more of the town of Mexico Beach?

I can't rely on Rudy's pickled brain to act rationally and I can't know if they've already picked up Carl and are heading back or if they haven't even made it yet. They could be on either stretch of road, and needing to find them as quickly as possible, I don't have time to get it wrong.

I pray for guidance and to be directed down the right path and to find them as quickly as possible, alive and well.

While I'm praying I glance at my phone again. Still no service.

The relentless sound of the wind and rain and the constant assault of the water and debris on my car are merciless and maddening. It makes me want to yell and hit something, and I wonder how Rudy is handling it.

As I approach the turnoff I decide to take it.

It's possible that Rudy missed it or went the long way for any number of irrational reasons, but the weather had to be getting bad when he was coming through and he would want to get his brother and get out of here as quickly as possible. It may be a mistake but I'm going with the most direct route possible, hoping he had enough wits about him to do the same.

As soon as I turn onto 15th Street and head for 98 and the west end of the town, I encounter another level of intensification—stronger winds, more rain, and far more challenges on the road.

Joining the limbs and leaves, branches and tree tops are pieces and parts of homes.

Shingles, insulation, and siding fly about like bits of

paper in the breeze above a trash fire, swirling, twisting, striking over objects.

Sheets of aluminum and tin ripped off homes, buildings, sheds, trailers, and RVs are tossed about like silver confetti, scraping their way across the road, stabbing and cutting trees and poles and other buildings, spearing the wet ground and standing straight up until another gust of wind snatches them out and flings them into something else.

Lengths of chain-link fence, some with the poles still attached to them, whip and wave in the wind as they're flung to and fro several yards away from where they once stood.

Interspersed within the roar of the wind and the gush of the rain I can hear the cracks and snaps of trees and light poles and beams and boards, the rips and tears of roofs and siding and walls, the thuds and dings and bangs of solid, heavy, flying objects crashing into others.

My car is taking extensive damage, debris striking it hard in all directions.

Something small and sharp hurled with tremendous velocity makes a hole in my windshield, tiny fissures in the glass spiderwebbing out from it, running toward each edge.

The day is so dark, the sheets of rain so thick, most of the objects blowing by are just unrecognizable shapes and masses, slightly darker than the background. But occasionally something comes by that I recognize.

A boat on the ground rolls across the road and into the ditch on the other side. A mostly intact shed slides diagonally while several feet above it a large section of roofing—plywood, felt, shingles and all—floats like a makeshift raft on a swift water current.

On either side of the street trees are falling into homes, crashing through windows, caving in large portions of roofs and falling into the rooms beneath them, crushing vehicles in yards—cars, trucks, golf carts.

In one yard around the base of a tree it looks as if the ground is bubbling up. When the tree finally falls I can see that it was the root system pushing up on the ground, lifting the grass to hang from the upturned roots like wet rugs hanging from a clothesline.

Trampolines in trees.

RVs on their sides.

Boats capsized in yards—many with their trailers still attached.

A campground in which all the campers are piled up on each other like a child's discarded toys.

Roofs lifting and falling over and over until finally they are ripped free and fly away.

Furniture and appliances in yards and on the sides of the road, a recliner tumbling end over end, a huge flatscreen sliding across the road as if on ice.

Everything I'm witnessing is surreal, as if on the other side of my windshield is a movie screen playing a big budget disaster flick instead of the actual all-too-real world.

As my windshield continues to creak and groan like it might break at any moment, an object, maybe a brick or a fire poker, strikes one of my wipers and knocks it off, leaving only the metal frame to scratch that side of the windshield. The noise it makes is a constant high-pitched shriek like nails on a chalkboard, and if the relentless roar of the wind and incessant slap of the rain didn't drive me mad this definitely will, but I can't turn my wipers off because I need the one remaining in order to see at all.

15th has never seemed so long before, and though the storm and the damage it has already caused is disorienting, I can tell I'm still quite a distance from Highway 98.

I continue on through the barrage of flying debris and falling trees, moving far more slowly than I would like but moving nonetheless—until all my forward progress comes to a dead stop.

35

There in the road, blocking both lanes and then some is a fallen, 100-foot-long loblolly pine tree, its thick body at least three feet in diameter.

There's no way for the car to get around it. The ditches on each side are too deep and the tree is covering one of them completely anyway.

I place the car in Park and look around to see if any other options exist.

Nothing obvious presents itself.

I should've stayed on Overstreet until it dead-ended into 98.

It's probably just as blocked.

Maybe, but fewer trees up there so . . .

But more homes and buildings and the storm surge.

Where are my girls? Are they at least in some form of shelter?

I can't stop. I've got to figure out a way around or . . . something.

What to do. What to do. What to do.

Time is wasting. The storm is intensifying and they're out there in it.

Do something. Anything.

I look to see if there's a back road that might get me around it and out on the other side of it. There's nothing obvious.

As far as I can see there are no driveways, subdivisions, or any way to get around the tree.

As I see it I have two options—turn around and search for a different route or leave the car here and go on foot, attempting to find another on the other side.

Since finding one with the keys in it is such a long shot, I turn the car around and head back in the direction I've just come from—which is already filled with more trash, trees, and debris.

The first side street I come to is California Drive. I take a right on it, then make my way around the dirty and soggy siding and boards and furniture and appliances until I come to Maryland Boulevard. Taking a right onto it I follow it the short distance down to Texas Drive and then, taking a right on Texas, stay on it all the way back to

15th and find that I am on the other side of the fallen loblolly.

Picking back up where I left off, I continue down 15th Street, dodging as best I can all the wreckage and rubble that is only increasing, trying to focus as best I can on the task at hand and not the metal wiper screeching on the windshield.

A front door flies by in front of me. Followed by a wooden kitchen chair and a wedding dress.

The wind seems to change directions and intensify and it sounds like the Sunset Limited rocking down the line, its whistle steadily blowing as if warning pedestrians off the track.

Wonder what Anna is doing right now. She has to be sick with worry, furious with frustration. Is she without power and cell service as well? Does she feel as isolated as I do?

Please protect us all—especially our children—and bring us all back together safely again.

All around me trees are falling, houses are breaking up and flying apart, all while the driving, windswept rain beats down upon everything.

A golf cart on its side suddenly appears in front of me and I brake and swerve but still manage to clip it pretty good. My car shimmies and nearly goes off the road as I attempt to right it.

A series of long but narrow slash pines have fallen across the road in quick succession and since I don't see that I have any other option I decide to go over the tops of them.

Giving the car more gas, I lunge headlong into the wet, loud, darkness, clacking across the tops of the pines as if on an uneven old railroad tie bridge, the branches and pine needles rubbing and brushing and scraping the undercarriage of the car.

Eventually, I reach the end of 15th Street and see that things are far worse here on Highway 98 among the beachfront homes, cottages, restaurants, and hotels that have no barrier between them and the direct and brutal assault of a true superstorm.

I glance around unable to comprehend the enormity of the power or the scope of the devastation, then take a right onto 98 in the direction of the marina and Carl's old fishing shack.

I don't get far.

My car is struck hard in the front driver's side and spun around, snapping my neck and slamming my head into the window.

I lose control of the car and it continues to spin around, hydroplaning off the highway and falling sideways into a sinkhole, water and sand filling in around me.

36

Blood drips into my eyes and I can taste it like wet pennies in my mouth.

With even the slightest moves I make, I can feel the car shift, sinking deeper down into the wet, quicksand-like substance of the hole.

Through the driver's side window I can see that a huge chunk of the highway has broken off and is partially in the hole. At least two of my car's tires are on it.

The vehicle is still running, the metal of the bald wiper still etching a half-moon into fractured glass.

Slowly, carefully, I reach down and turn off the engine and stop the maddening sound of metal scratching glass.

The car shifts again and I can feel the ground moving beneath me.

Massive amounts of water sluices along the contours of the car and continues to fill the hole.

I've got to climb out of the car as quickly and carefully as possible.

I reach down and press the button to release my seatbelt and hold it as it retracts, guiding it slowly back onto its spool.

Wonder what hit me. It was big and coming fast.

Feeling my way along the door I find the door lock button and unlock the doors.

Now, how to climb free without causing the car to plunge deeper into a chasm I won't be able to claw my way out of.

Deciding that even if opening the door is an option, which with the damage to the car it's probably not, it will cause too much movement and pressure on the vehicle, I realize that my best chance of escape is to roll down the window and climb out through it.

With my right hand I reach down and turn the car back on, the screeching wiper starting back up again, while with my left I press the button on the door that rolls down the window.

Water immediately starts pouring into the car and I can tell it won't be long before the weight of it causes the car to shift and fall farther into the sinkhole.

Turning quickly in my seat, I put my feet on the center console and my hands on the outside edges of the window frame of the door and push and pull up simultaneously, the car shifting as I do.

Stepping from the console to the door frame, the car shifting and sliding more as I do, I stand on the side of the car, one foot on each side of the open window, searching for something to grab—anything I can hold on to and use to pull myself up.

The wall of asphalt is wet and slick and offers nothing to grasp—except at the very top edge where it has separated from the rest of the road.

I reach up for it, the car sinking beneath me, but find that I am about eight inches too low to be able to grab it.

You've got to jump.

But it'll cause the car to fall farther down the hole so you'll probably only get once chance.

Make it count.

I glance around quickly for any other options and seeing none, I ready myself to jump up and grab the jagged edge of the huge section of blacktop.

Bending my knees, I'm about to spring up as if taking a jump shot when I hear something.

"Hey. Are you okay?" a young frightened male voice says.

He is yelling but I can barely hear him over the roar of the wind and the pounding of the rain.

I look up to see two early twenties identical twin guys with blond hair darkened by the rain, big blue eyes, and dramatic features that will benefit from the filling out adulthood and weight gain will bring.

"So sorry we hit you, dude. Can't see for shit out here."

"Here, grab my hand and we'll pull you up."

I reach up and each of them takes one of my hands in both of theirs and they lift as I push up on the car, the relentless rain beating down on us, the whipping, gusting wind buffeting our every move.

They pull me up onto the pavement and we all run for their vehicle to get out of the wind and rain and avoid the debris being blown about.

Their vehicle is a black F-250 with a crew cab, which I climb into the back of.

"Thank you," I say.

"Well, you're welcome, but we're sort of the ones who put you in there."

I can see that the huge truck is fitted with camera equipment—at least one camera mounted on every window.

"What're you guys doing out here?" I ask.

"Thought we wanted to be storm chasers, but fuck that."

"We're gettin' the hell up out of here."

"I'm Ethan," the driver says. "This is my brother Evan."

"John," I say.

"Well, John, whatta you say we get the hell out of here?"

He puts the truck in gear and begins to roll away from the spot where my car is sinking.

"I say I can't. And actually I need your help to go get—"

"Let me rephrase," he says. "We're gettin' the hell up outta here. This shit is far, far worse than anyone thought it was going to be. If you stay in this vehicle you'll be moving away from the storm at a rapid rate of speed."

"I'm afraid I can't let you do that," I say. I pull out my badge and ID and show it to them. "I'm an investigator with the Gulf County Sheriff's Department and I'm commandeering this vehicle."

"*What*?" Ethan says.

"*Whoa*," Evan says.

"No," Ethan says.

"Sorry," I say. "But I have to."

"Do you have a gun?" Evan asks.

"I do," I say. "Why?"

"No reason."

"I could really use your help," I say, "but if you like I can drop you off somewhere."

"*Where*?" Ethan says.

"Yeah," Evan adds, "where the hell would you drop us off?"

"You could get into one of the structures still standing."

"Fuck that," Evan says. "We'll take our chances with you."

"Where are we going?" Ethan says. "What is it that you want us to do?"

"Someone took my children," I say. "They're down close to the marina."

"Your own kids? Really?"

"That sounds sus—"

"Yeah. He's in an old red Cadillac. He came to pick up his brother who lives down by the marina. Mind if I drive?"

37

"Just be careful," Ethan says. "It's our dad's truck and he doesn't know we have it."

He puts the truck in Park and climbs into the backseat.

I climb behind the wheel, throw the truck into gear, and gun it.

"Easy," Evan says.

"Where are you guys from?" I ask.

It's so loud even inside the truck that we have to raise our voices in order to hear each other.

"Albany, Georgia," Evan says.

"Which is where our dumb asses should be right now," Ethan says. "Fuckin' storm chasers. What the fuck were we thinkin'?"

The truck vibrates like the tires are out of balance, but it's wind and the wet road.

To our right, half a semi tractor trailer slides in a pizza place parking lot, its rippling edges jagged where it had been ripped in two. Neither of the twins notice it.

"It's nothin' like on TV," Evan says.

"We're too young to die in this shit," Ethan says.

"Well, let's make sure that doesn't happen," I say. "How long y'all been in town?"

"Got here last night," Ethan says.

"Yeah, back when this bitch was supposed to be a Category 1 or 2," Evan adds.

"What have you seen?"

"Some scary fuckin' shit," Evan says. "This little town is gettin' leveled and we haven't even had the storm surge yet."

In the truck's headlights the windswept rain seems to slither along the pavement like the apparition of a long-dead prehistoric reptile.

"Seen anyone else around?" I ask.

"Yeah, a few real storm chasers and TV weather people."

The tops of the planted palm trees lining the beach side of the road look to be rag dolls being throttled by a violent and angry child.

"No one in a red Cadillac?" I ask.

"Hey," Evan says. "What kind of car was that down in that—"

"We only saw the back of it," Ethan says, "but it coulda been a Cadillac."

"Where?" I ask. "Down in what?"

"Beside one of the condos up there," he says, nodding in the direction we're heading. "There's this drop-off down into drainage ditch or something. A car is nose down in it standing almost straight up."

"Show me," I say.

Above us, crisscrossing the road, some of the power lines jangle, playing tug-of-war between the poles still standing. Still others have snapped and are whipping about wildly. Some of the poles have splintered and broken and lie on the ground, while the upper half of others dangle from the lines still connected to them.

"It may not be red or a Cadillac," Ethan says. "It's hard to tell in all this shit—even earlier before it got this bad."

"It's in the right direction," I say. "Won't cost us anything to look."

"'Cept maybe our lives," Evan says.

We continue on as more and bigger objects swirl all around and into us. It seems as though, in an attempt to stop us, an unseen force is actually hurling things at us. They come with such velocity that they're difficult to dodge.

I zigzag around a large dumpster, an RV on its side, a

nearly complete intact roof and then a truck with a golf cart through its windshield.

All the while the wind howls and hisses and screams, the rain slashes and spits and smacks.

To our left most of the doors and windows and some of the walls of a hotel are gone. It would look like a giant dollhouse with cutaways to see inside if it weren't for the trash and debris and rubble spilling out of it.

Nearly everywhere you look, trees and light poles are not only down but are also sticking out of houses and buildings and vehicles as if spears thrown by a giant angry sea creature.

Piles and piles of two-by-fours and trusses and other framing boards are scattered about like discarded match-sticks at a busy cigar bar. Next to, underneath, and on top of them are the colorful awnings and beachy print curtains and drapes and bedspreads and rugs that once decorated serene Gulfside getaways enjoyed by genera-tions of vacationers from Georgia, Alabama, and Tennessee.

Mixed among the board-and-cinder-block rubble, as if awaiting discovery by an archeological dig one day, are the large and small fragments of terra cotta pots, colorful porcelain tiles, painted cement pelicans, and a million, trillion other parts and pieces of seaside decorations from the chic to the kitschy—in the sand, on the streets, anywhere but in the homes and hotel rooms they used to adorn.

"There," Ethan says. "Down in there."

"Okay," I say. "Let's go check it out."

"Can't we just wait here?" Evan asks.

"You might decide to leave me," I say.

"Take the key."

"You may have another."

I can tell by the glance between them that they do.

"Let's have it," I say. "And you're still coming with me."

Ethan produces another key to the vehicle and I put both in my pocket.

"We're talking about my children, guys," I say. "I'll do whatever I have to to find them. Don't test me."

"Sorry, man," Ethan says. "We're just scared."

"And we don't know you, man," Evan says. "You could be lying about all of it."

"Well, I'm not," I say. "And if you won't believe me, believe my gun. Now, let's go."

38

We climb out of the truck and are immediately drenched again.

The wind catches the door and jerks it out of my hand and I have to go on the other side of it and push on it with all my strength and weight to get it to close.

It sounds like a freight train is barreling down on us.

And swirling all around within the roar of the storm is the incessant bleating of innumerable home and car alarms.

Twisted pieces of tin roofing are batted about all around us, snapping, popping, rippling loudly. So are studs with nails protruding from them and partial sheets of plywood.

These and the other debris flying around us are

dangerous, many of them sharp and heavy, and we move over toward the spot they have indicated in crouched positions with our hands held up defensively.

It's hard to hear anything above the wind. It's hard to see anything apart from the rain.

Bits of sand and rock and unidentifiable trash hit my face and hands like birdshot from a shotgun.

Between the deafening volume of the storm and its merciless physical assault it feels like a brutal and effective form of torture. I can feel the jagged, fringy ends of my nerves fraying even more, a maddening in my mind, a rage in my core, and I can't imagine what it's doing to my precious little girls.

By the time we near the area, which takes a lot longer than it normally would, I realize that Evan is not with us.

"Where is Evan?" I yell.

"Got hit by a piece of metal," Ethan yells back. "Got back in the truck to bandage it. It's down there."

He points to a place just past the retaining wall on this side of a drainage ditch between the front edge of a three-story condo and storm water runoff bridge.

I rush up to it and look over.

There, nose down in the rising water, standing nearly straight up with a thick, wooden creosote-treated power pole through it, is Rudy's red Cadillac.

We're looking down at the back of the car, the bumper, trunk, back tires, and the back windshield with the light pole sticking out of it, and though the top of the pole extends up much higher, the back of the car is about four feet below where we're standing.

The water comes up to about the halfway mark of the front door but is rising fast.

Without really thinking, I jump down into the water.

Already completely soaked through several times over, I don't attempt to remove any clothing or my shoes.

Down in the drainage ditch the rain is just as heavy but a bit of the wind is blocked by the cement walls.

As I work to open the door, a light comes on behind me that illuminates me and the door.

I turn to look and see that Ethan has a video camera with a large light on it recording. He yells something but I can't make it out. All I hear is wind and rain and the bashing and smashing of buildings and the blood coursing heavily through my ears.

I open the door thinking of all the ways I'm going to bring pain, misery, and death down upon Rudy if Johanna, Taylor, or John Paul are injured or . . . But I find the front seat empty apart from the large power pole extending down through the dashboard and into the engine.

I push myself up to get on the open door so I can see into the backseat.

"What is it?" Ethan yells. "What do you see?"

The backseat is empty too—leaving me to wonder what happened and where they could be.

Were they in the car when it went into the water? Did they get out? Were they rescued? Are they at a hospital or shelter right now? Or were they already out of the car when it went in? Are they in Carl's house? His car? Another vehicle? Somewhere else? Is it possible they're somewhere safe and dry?

Hard to imagine with Rudy running things.

"How're you gonna get back up here?" Ethan yells.

I look around. Built like a narrow cement canal, there's no obvious or good way back up.

Deciding my best and maybe only way back up is on the car, I climb onto the roof and slide along the back windshield, carefully avoiding the power pole, and then up the trunk until I'm standing on the bumper—from which I grab the top part of the retaining wall and pull myself up with some help from Ethan.

"Come on," he says. "We've got to get back in the truck."

I look around the area again. And seeing no signs of Taylor, Johanna, or John Paul, make my way back to the truck.

Back inside the truck—this time with Ethan in the passenger seat and Evan in the back—completely soaked and sore, skin stinging, ears ringing and popping, I sit still for a moment, collecting myself, breathing deeply and slowly.

"You okay?" Ethan asks Evan.

"Yeah. Guess it scared me more than anything else. Man, I was freakin' the fuck out. Sorry I bailed."

"All good, brah," Ethan says. "Don't sweat it."

I crank the truck and turn on the wipers.

He looks over at me. "Do you feel the pressure falling again? The worst of it is almost here. I bet we're about to get sustained winds over 155 and gusts over 200 with far more storm surge. We've got to get out of here. Hopefully, they made it to safety. But either way you're not going to be any good to them dead."

"I've got to check the place they were headed," I say. "It's not much farther up this way."

"Hurry, man. Please. I know they're your kids, but . . . we're somebody's kids too and . . ."

"We don't want to die," Evan says. "Please."

While they've been talking, I've been scanning the area as best I can in the headlights between wiper swipes. With no sign of the kids, I put the truck into gear and begin to head in the direction of Carl's little fishing shack.

We haven't gone far when more of the storm surge comes in and every aspect of the storm intensifies.

"*Ho-ly* fuck," Evan says as the giant wall of water rolls in. "We're all gonna die."

39

The wave is enormous and stretches inland for longer than seems possible.

What once was beach and dunes and houses and restaurants and road is now Gulf.

It is as if we are suddenly at sea and the F-250 is a boat instead of a truck. Now in addition to debris flying around in the wind it is also being pushed around by the water.

Vehicles, what looks to be the entire contents of houses, and houses themselves are now floating about, bobbing up and down in the undulating water as they are tossed to and fro, swept from side to side by what looks to have the power of a riptide.

If the kids are in this how can they still be alive?

There's a good chance none of you are going to survive this. This isn't survivable.

"Drive faster," Ethan says.

"Fuck that," Evan says. "Turn down a side road and drive as fast as you can away from this shit."

There's genuine panic in his voice and I wonder how long it will be before he freaks out to the point of becoming a problem.

"We're close," I say. "And we're not stopping. Take some deep breaths and try to calm down. Panicking isn't going to help anything."

"Fuck you, man. You steal our damn truck and have us out here in this shit so we can die alongside you and you tell me to take some breaths and calm down. Fuck you."

"Evan, dude," Ethan says. "We're gonna be okay. I promise, brah. Nothing's gonna happen to the wonder twins tonight. God won't let it. Just chill."

"Is that a . . ." Evan says, staring out the window in wide-eyed shock. "It is. That's a fuckin' house floating down the road—an entire fuckin' house. Why aren't you two freaking out? What is wrong with you? That's a house —*a house*—floating down the street."

"We're almost there," I say. "Just a little bit farther."

"How can you tell?" Evan asks. "There's nothing but water. How long before it floods the engine and we drown out here or it sucks us back out to sea? I'm serious. This is absolutely fuckin' nuts, what we're doing."

We move along the flooded highway as fast as possible, trying to dodge the floating debris, the water high enough in some places to lift the vehicle and turn it slightly.

Eventually, we reach the road Carl's little fishing hut is on and I turn in.

Carl's small place is a throwback to when Mexico Beach was less touristy and more a place where locals actually lived. Rudy had told me several times that Carl has been offered insane amounts of money for his property but had always refused to sell, that he likes having an old wooden one-room fishing shack next to million dollar beach mansions.

Parking the truck, I jump out and—I feel like I'm in a war zone.

I thought the roar of the wind couldn't get any louder but now it is. It's as if we went from a freight train racing toward us to the runway of a busy metropolitan airport. I feel like my head is directly behind a jet engine at full throttle.

Visibility is now at near zero. As if a snowstorm instead of a hurricane, the wind and rain and fog create a near total whiteout.

Finding it difficult to walk, I lean into the wind and

wade through the water as best I can, but my forward progress is extremely slow. With my hands outstretched I'm feeling my way more than anything else, only able to see objects once I'm right up on them.

Suddenly, Ethan is beside me.

He's yelling something about helping me find my kids, but I can't make out much of it.

I yell *Thank you* and give him a thumbs up signal but I'm not sure he receives either.

We lock arms and help each other stumble and fall forward.

It takes us a while to make it just a few feet, but when we get to the place where Carl's little cottage is supposed to be, it's gone.

I feel like crying but scream profanities into the swirling whirlwind instead as all around me the sea is coming ashore and washing away the town.

"Come on," Ethan yells. "We've got to get back to the truck."

"I've got to look around some more," I yell back. "The house could be close by and they could still be in it."

" . . . point . . . best . . . do . . . out . . . storm . . . truck. Look . . . after . . ."

He grabs my arm and begins to pull me toward the truck, but I shrug his hand off and move in the opposite direction.

The only thing I know for sure is that I'm moving

away from him. I have no idea what direction I'm actually moving in.

Then I stop for a moment as I have a thought.

If the wind blew Carl's little place away, there's nothing I can do, but if the tide lifted and floated it away then all I have to do is follow the current of the water.

I bend down to try to see which way the water is flowing and then begin to follow it as best I can.

"At least . . . keys . . . don't . . . kill . . . us too," Ethan is yelling behind me.

I start to shout at him how and why I can't, but before I can I hear what sounds like faint screams in the dim distance.

I turn my head back toward Ethan slightly.

"Did you hear that?" I yell.

"What?"

"Screams."

" . . . just . . . wind. Come . . ."

I continue toward the direction I believe I heard the screams coming from, hoping he will follow me.

I've only taken a few steps when I'm struck on the back of the head by something hard and heavy and I pitch forward into the water.

Suddenly Ethan is there behind me, holding me down with one hand while reaching into my pocket and withdrawing one of the truck keys with the other.

" . . . save . . . brother. Sorry."

I struggle to get free and stand up and he doesn't fight me.

When I'm upright again he is gone and in the whiteout I can't tell how far or in which direction.

I hear something that may be "Sorry" in the wind but can't be sure.

I continue in the direction I believe the screams came from, not knowing for sure it's the right direction or if I even heard them in the first place.

But what else can I do?

I can't stop. I can't quit searching for the little beings that are so precious to me, that I would gladly give my life for.

I hit my shin on something hard and metal beneath the water, maybe a fire hydrant, and while the pain from it is still vibrating through me, trip over something that might be a curb.

And then I hear the screams again.

Or maybe it's just the roaring, whistling, howling, shrieking wind.

It could be. I could be out here blindly following voices out of Job's whirlwind while my children are in peril somewhere else. I just can't know.

Until.

Out of the deafening, maddening, screaming storm I hear one word.

"Daddy."

And then I know with the certainty that only a parent can have, that of all the little girls in all the world that was *my* little girl calling me.

40

It's the sweetest sound I've ever heard—and it comes in the midst of some of the most vicious and violent and savage noises my ears have ever been subjected to.

"Daddy," Johanna screams again. "Help us. Please, Daddy."

I move faster, sloshing through the water, holding my hands up and out to both feel my way and protect myself from flying objects.

Eventually, my hands feel the wood siding of Carl's old fishing shack.

"Daddy," Johanna screams again. "Daddy. Daddy. Please. Please."

"Johanna, Taylor, I'm here," I yell back. "I'm here, baby. Daddy's here."

The small wooden structure is floating upside down in the water. It bobs up and down with the tide but it's not moving back and forth much. It must be lodged against another structure or trees on the other side.

It's creaking and groaning and boards are flying off it. I can't imagine it won't be very long before it either flies apart or collapses. And my little girls are inside of it.

Grabbing the corner bobbing up and down, I pull myself up onto the unstable structure and crawl up to a broken window at the center of the side wall, boards ripping off and blowing away all around me as I do.

When I reach the opening and look inside, I break down and start sobbing.

There sitting on the ceiling in water up to her neck, floating furniture and trash all around her, Johanna holds an unconscious Taylor, Taylor's small head lying on Johanna's tiny shoulder.

Not far from them, Carl's body floats facedown in the water between an oven and an overturned couch.

There is no sign of Rudy or John Paul.

"Are you okay, Daddy?" Johanna asks.

"I'm just so glad I found you," I say.

Parts of the old shack are falling off inside as well, some of them landing very close to Johanna and Taylor. How long will it be before one hits them?

"I can't hold her up much longer," she says.

"I'll be down there in just a minute," I say. "I love you so much. I'm so proud of you, big girl. You're amazing."

"I'm so glad you're here, Daddy," she says.

"I am too, baby. I am too."

I twist around and lower my body into the building, holding myself by the window frame.

"I'm gonna have to drop in," I say. "It's going to make a splash, okay?"

"Okay, Daddy."

"Just keep holding on."

"I will, Daddy."

"On three," I say. "One. Two. Three."

I let go and drop the fifteen feet or so down into the water not far from Carl, my ankle turning on the uneven surface beneath.

I rush over to them, sloshing and splashing as I do, and take them both into my arms.

I feel another level of relief as I feel Taylor breathing.

I examine her as best I can and try to wake her. She has a bump on the left side of her head that doesn't appear to be too bad and she opens her eyes slightly when I pat her on the shoulder and say her name. Her pupils are the same size and appear normal. For now, I'll let her sleep, and try to wake her and keep her up after we find a safer place to hole up.

Outside boards continue to blow off. Inside they continue to drop, some of them landing very near us.

"You're the bravest girl I know," I say to Johanna. "I am so proud of you."

"Thank you, Daddy. I'm so glad you're here. Mr. Rudy just left us."

"Are you okay?"

She nods her little head. "Just wet and tired and sore from holding Taylor."

"How long has she been out?"

She shrugs. "I don't know exactly, Daddy. She bumped her head on a big board when the house turned over and started floating away."

"Did it knock her out or was she awake a while before she went to sleep?"

"Awake a while."

"Did she throw up or say her head hurt?"

"No, sir."

"Does Rudy have John Paul?"

"Yes, sir, but he left us."

"Makes me want to kill him," I say.

"Don't do that, Daddy," she says. "But you can beat him up if you want to."

The house shifts and turns and feels like it might be about to break free from whatever has been holding it stationary. This causes even more of the inner walls and floor planks to break off and fall around us.

"We need to get out of here," I say, looking around. "It's not safe."

It's not, but neither is out there in the storm.

Halfway up on the wall across from us is the front door. It's open and lying horizontally with the new orientation of the upside-down house, but it looks too high for us to get up to.

A window that was once beside it and is now below it might work for our escape.

I wade over to it, one girl in each arm.

"It's really horrible out there," I say, "but I don't think it's safe to stay in here. We'll try to find another, safer structure to get into until the storm passes, okay?"

"Okay, Daddy."

"You're such a brave girl," I say. "I've always been so proud of you, but never more than right now. You saved your and your sister's lives."

The old wooden structure shifts again and more of it falls inside and flies off outside.

"Thank you, Daddy."

"Once we get outside I'm gonna put you on my back and strap you to me with my belt," I say, "but I'm gonna need you to hold on to me with all your might. Okay? I know you're tired and sore but it's really important. Don't let go. Feel free to close your eyes if you want to but don't cover your ears. Keep your hands wrapped around me. Okay?"

"Okay, Daddy. I will."

The glass of the windows has been blown out, but jagged shards remain sticking up out of the frame.

"Can I put you down for a second?" I ask.

She nods.

"I need to find something to . . ."

I see a wooden kitchen chair floating nearby and grab it.

"Need me to hold Taylor?" Johanna asks.

"Do you mind?"

"No, sir. Not at all."

I gently place Taylor in her arms, then use the chair to knock the rest of the glass out of the frame. When that's done, I look around until I find something to put down over it. Finding a few floating pillows, I place them on the old aluminum frame to cover any glass I missed.

"Okay," I say. "Here we go. Come over here as close as you can to the window. I'll climb through. You can pass me Taylor, then I'll help you climb through."

She gives me a slight nod, but doesn't say anything.

"You okay?"

She nods but it's not convincing.

"What is it? What's wrong?"

"I just don't want to go out into that," she says.

"Me either, but—and we wouldn't if I thought it was safe in here."

"I know, Daddy. It's okay. I'm ready."

"Okay. Stay real close so I can grab you if I need to."

I see part of the sub flooring falling above us and quickly grab Johanna and Taylor and pull them in front of me and arch my back and bend over them. The board is big and heavy and hits both my back and the back of my head. I'm staggered and dazed a bit but manage to stay on my feet and keep the girls from harm.

"You okay?" I ask Johanna when I can.

"Yeah, just scared me."

"Let's get out of here," I say.

I quickly climb out then reach for Taylor, then with one arm help Johanna out.

And now, with no vehicle and no shelter, no help and no hope, I am out in the apocalyptic-like superstorm of the century with my two little girls.

41

Clinging to Taylor in the front with one hand and to Johanna who is strapped to my back with a belt with the other, I wade through the water slowly and carefully because going any faster would risk tripping and falling and injuring the girls.

Not that I could go much faster anyway. Not with the weight of the girls and the force of the storm.

Because I have the girls, the assault of the rain and the wallop of the wind feel even more brutal and personal.

I can feel Johanna's little face pressed hard against my back and I'm glad it is, though I wish there was a way to protect her ears from the noise and her head and body from the pelting rain and debris.

I'm not sure how far we've walked or in which direction, but I nearly step into a swimming pool that already has a white Honda Accord and a red moped in it.

As I change directions to walk around it and blink the rain out of my eyes, I see a large house on stilts—the only one in the area still standing.

All around it, the flattened landscape is covered with the remnants of other houses, but it looks nearly untouched, which can only mean one thing—someone exceeded code and built a hurricane house.

I begin to make my way toward it, allowing myself a faint sense of relief and a modicum of hope as I do.

As I get closer, I see lights and movement inside. Not the overhead lights and lamps that would indicate their generator is still working but the glow of lanterns and the play of flashlight beams that let us know help is inside.

In my hope and excitement I begin to walk too fast and trip and nearly fall, but even as I try to slow down some I find it difficult to return to my earlier more cautious pace.

"Johanna," I yell, "I found a safe place for us to go into to get out of the wind and rain."

Without moving her face away from my back, she nods to let me know she's heard me, a moment later pumping her little arms in celebration.

Taylor begins to stir, and though I'm sure she's going to be frightened and disoriented waking in the middle of the pummel and pounding of the storm, I'll be very glad to have her conscious again.

I continue to move toward the lone structure as if I'm a ship lost at sea and it's a lighthouse leading me home.

For a moment it disappears and I think maybe I've imagined it, that it is the storm equivalent of a desert mirage, but then the wind slashes in a different direction and my rain-impaired vision clears enough to see it again.

"We're almost there," I yell. "Just a little bit—"

I stop abruptly—speaking and moving.

Not far from the house now, I have a better view, and can see through the large bay window in the front.

A man with a hood over his head is bound and bleeding. Tied to a wooden kitchen chair, he is being worked over by one man while another one holds a shotgun to his head.

I recognize the two men inflicting the torture from the suspicious group at Ace the other day with the stolen van that I had seen the burned body in this morning.

Ordinarily I would feel compelled to intervene, to sneak up into the house and attempt to rescue the man being tortured, but my first and only priority right now is the care and protection of my girls. That is all that matters. They are all that matter.

Rousing now, Taylor begins to cry.

I can barely hear her over the cacophony of the storm, so I'm reasonably sure the men in the house can't hear her, but I need to get her and Johanna as far away from the house and the men in it as fast as I can.

I begin to slowly back away, keeping an eye on the window to make sure they don't see us, though how they could through the wind and rain I can't imagine.

As I continue to back up, I not only keep an eye on them, but search the area for somewhere safe for us to hide and ride out the rest of the storm.

I'm wondering how far away we have to get to be safe, when I spot it.

42

There in the distance is an old capsized cabin cruiser.

It's not as far away from the men as I'd like but there's nothing else even close and we've got to get out of the storm. When it passes and we can move again, we'll get farther away from them.

I get us over to it as quickly as possible, Taylor beginning to cry more loudly and squirm more violently.

The bow of the boat is wedged between a palm tree and a concrete piling and doesn't appear to be going anywhere.

The inside of the old upside-down boat is wet and sandy and filled with smelly seaweed and debris, but it gets us out of the wind and rain.

I crawl as far back into it as I can, unstrap Johanna from my back, and put one girl on each leg and hold them to me tightly. Withdrawing my weapon, I place it on the floor next to me so I can get to it quickly if I need to.

Both Johanna and I work at calming Taylor down, and after trying everything else it is the promise of ice cream after the storm passes that finally works.

We are all exhausted—drained and depleted emotionally, mentally, and physically—hot, wet, sticky, sore, hungry, thirsty, and generally miserable. But we are together and alive and out of the direct thrashing of the storm.

I sing softly to the girls and tell them stories, but not for long. Soon they are both sound asleep, each of them twitching and breathing erratically, probably the first of many signs of hurricane-induced PTSD.

For the first time in a long time I am able to think about something other than finding my children.

I wonder how Anna is—besides worried about us. Is she safe? Alive? How hard was Wewa hit? I hope she stayed home and didn't try to come out looking for us.

How is John Paul? Where is he? Is he okay? Alive? It's hard to imagine he could be, given who he was with and what he was out in, but for the moment, since I can't afford to break down, I'm going to trust that he is alive and well and that we'll all be together again soon. What else can I do, given my current circumstance and situation?

How are things at the sheriff's department and the prison?

I feel so isolated and alone, so cut off from the rest of the world, and I wonder if maybe everyone in the area is experiencing the same thing. With a storm this powerful there's a good chance that everyone from Panama City to Port St. Joe to Wewa is without communications, electricity, and at best inside damaged structures surrounded by trees and debris—truly separated from each other and the rest of the world.

There's no question that the coastal areas are taking the hardest hit, but a superstorm this strong and devastating will do catastrophic destruction a good distance inland as well.

I'm so grateful to have my girls in my arms, to be here with them, holding them while they sleep, and of all the heroic feats that an event like this will no doubt give rise to, I can't imagine anyone being more brave or heroic than Johanna. Thinking of what she went through and what she did for her sister simultaneously breaks my heart and fills it with immense pride.

Even as I'm holding Johanna and Taylor and thinking all these things, I keep picturing the men from the house or Andrew's killer appearing at the entrance of the boat, and I occasionally reach down and touch my weapon to make sure it's still there.

The boat rocks back and forth some, its old boards creaking and groaning, but it never floats away and it never breaks apart.

And eventually, the storm passes.

It's difficult to fathom but in the same way it blew in, the storm blows out. The rain stops and the wind dies down and the calm before the storm returns. And just like that, this moving apocalypse is gone, this existential phenomenon that has changed us and our home forever is just gone.

I wait a long while before even thinking of climbing out of the boat, and it's not until I hear a few voices and vehicles and dogs barking that I chance it.

"Hey," I say to the girls. "It's over. The storm is gone. I'm going to crawl out and make sure it's safe. Y'all stay here for just a minute while I do. Okay? As soon as I'm certain it's safe I'll help you out."

"Don't go far, Daddy." Johanna says. "Don't leave us."

"I would never. I'll stand right there at the edge so you can see me the whole time. Okay? And I'll only be a minute."

She nods. "Okay."

"I promise I would never leave you," I say.

"I know."

"Would you mind holding Taylor for me while I make sure it's safe for y'all?"

"No, Daddy. I don't mind."

After holstering my gun, I help her off my lap and get her situated beside me and then ease Taylor into her little lap.

"Best big sister ever," I say.

43

Mexico Beach is no more.

The small coastal town has been obliterated, nearly completely leveled.

Very few structures remain standing and of those, nearly all are severely damaged.

I'm standing in quiet and calm I wouldn't have thought possible just an hour ago. It's warm and wet, the quality of the air far more tropical than before the storm. Occasional raindrops splat the already damp pavement and a gentle breeze rustles the branches of downed trees and loose house wrap, but it's mostly silent and serene, which given what we've just experienced and the destruction left behind, is surreal.

Wet trash and debris are everywhere.

Highway 98 is completely missing in places, the rest

of it filled with sand and rubble and entire houses that floated off their foundations and settled on the road when the tide went back out.

The beautiful beach, with its bright green waters and pristine white sand is now a dirty wasteland of rubbish, wreck, and ruin.

And it's flat.

All the powdery, sugary white dunes have been washes away—the beach, like the town, leveled.

The scope and scale of the devastation and destruction is scarcely imaginable.

Slowly the few souls who defied the evacuation order and stayed—and actually survived—begin to come out into the now post-apocalyptic landscape, surveying the desolate tropical desert with stunned disbelief while shaking heads and shedding tears.

I glance over at the hurricane house, which is not in the direction I thought it was, and see no vehicles or signs of life.

Though there aren't many people around, I believe it's probably enough that if the men from the house are still here, they won't try anything and it's safe to bring the girls out.

I wait just a few moments more, just to be certain, and as I do a deputy in a patrol car with his flashers on and a city worker in a white truck with yellow lights— also flashing—weave their way around, over, and through the scattered ruined raw materials of fifteen hundred homes.

When they get near I wave them over.

"John?" the deputy asks in shock. "The hell you doin' out here?"

He's a young, overly muscled white boy named Denny who fancies himself a badass—and just might be. Really hasn't been put to the test yet.

"It's a long story," I say. "What's the situation?"

"A couple of us rode it out at the fire station," he said. "Made it through alive, but . . . All communications are down—we got no landlines, no cell service, and no radio. And we're trapped. Trees blocking the roads in every direction. No way out or in. We're truly and utterly fucked. It just . . . doesn't seem real."

I nod and look around some more.

He shakes his head again and says, "Just . . . doesn't . . . seem . . . real."

"No, it doesn't. How many other officers we got down here?"

"Just one other—Freddy. Why?"

I give him a brief account of why I'm down here, what happened, and what I saw in the one intact house visible in the area around us.

"They're inside the boat?" he asks. "Are they okay?"

"I'd like to get them in your car and back to the fire-house," I say. "Then we can get Freddy, some Kevlar, and weapons and enter that house over there. Even if they're not in it, they're around here somewhere, trapped here like the rest of us."

Even as I'm saying it I realize that I won't be able to leave Johanna and Taylor—not even long enough to do that, and especially not to do something as dangerous as that. And it's not just because they wouldn't want me to. I don't want to leave them. I want to finish what I've started and get them back home safely—if we still have a home to get back to.

"Entering the house part won't be necessary," he says. "I was over there checking it out a few minutes ago. It's empty. The door was open, so I went in. Found the backdoor on the beach side open too. Searched the entire place. There's no one in it—not even the owners. No one. It's in a little disarray but not bad. I just figured it was the wind after the doors blew open. It possible you just imagined it—in the middle of the storm and all?"

"It's possible, I guess, but I don't think so."

"Well, let's get your girls back to the fire station and figure out our next move from there."

As I crawl in and get Johanna and Taylor out I hear Denny telling the handful of other residents to get back inside, that it's not safe out here.

"Get back inside what exactly?" one of the women asks.

44

———

It's later that evening—the evening of the day that has changed everything.

From now on, for the foreseeable future, everyone in this area will divide time along the fault line of before and after Michael.

Our lives have been permanently and unalterably altered.

I'm standing in front of the fire station with Johanna and Taylor watching a particularly peaceful and beautiful sunset beyond the flattened terrain at the horizon where Gulf and sky melt into one another.

The three of us have rehydrated from a Culligan water bottle inside the station and satiated our hunger as best we could with stale Saltines and jalapeño Vienna sausage that would have been too hot for the girls if they hadn't been more famished than any other time in their short lives.

After leaving the boat with Denny, we had driven back to the area where Rudy's car is and searched for John Paul. We hunted for him in other sections of town too—and enlisted the assistance of other law enforcement, firefighters, emergency services, and civilians—but we found no trace of him or Rudy.

Freddy and one of the young firemen are out looking for him now, but our best hope is he and Rudy got out somehow. I'm trying my best not to think about it much.

I want to be out there searching for him now, but I can't leave my girls. They've made me promise them that —and I don't want to be away from them anyway. Besides, what could I do in the dark with no vehicle? Still, it eats away at me, fills me with grief and guilt.

The evening is serene and restorative and I'm taking a moment to breathe it in before I return to our new dire reality.

Night is falling fast. We have no electricity. No real food or water to speak of. We have no idea what's going on in the world outside this one and no way to find out. We are trapped here with no real hope of help. Not only can anyone close by not get to us—any more than we could get to them—but chances are they are just as devastated as we are and are in need of assistance themselves.

I have two little girls who have already been through hell to look after and I have no resources to do so.

I miss Anna and the common comforts of our home and the familiar consolations of our family and friends. But mostly I miss Anna.

As we stand there in the silence that seems our most natural state in the past few hours, a tall, thin old fireman with thick gray stubble named Herman walks up to stand beside us.

"Be a while 'fore they gather all their data and crunch all their numbers," he says, "but I can tell you standing here right now that if that wasn't a Category 5 it was right at it."

"I think that's like saying 'this isn't the end of the world but you can see it from here,'" I say.

"Ah, yep. Most certainly is. If that's not the most powerful storm to hit the Panhandle and one of the most powerful hurricanes to hit the US, I'll eat my hard hat and my rubber boots. But I guarantee it was. Came up fast and hit us hard in the mouth too. Ah, yep, that was a sucker punch for sure. Kate. Andrew. Opal. Katrina. Michael put 'em all to shame. Just you wait and see."

"I'm convinced," I say.

I feel helpless and powerless, unable to get Johanna and Taylor home, no ability to properly provide for them here. And added to those feelings are guilt and frustration at not being able to do anything for Anna or Merrill or Dad and Verna or John Paul or do anything about the men that had been in the hurricane house.

All I can really do right now is be fully present with the girls and offer them comfort and care, and that's what I intend to do.

"Very few people on the planet have ever or will ever go through what we just did," he says.

"I envy them," I say.

"Ah, yep. 'Specially with little 'uns. Glad you were able to find them in time."

I continue to rub the girls' shoulders and this time squeeze them a little.

Before I can say anything, we hear a loud engine and the sound of trees falling and rolling and turn to see what it is.

Johanna and Taylor both tap my leg and indicate they want me to pick them up, which I do.

As we turn, we see the front end of a John Deere skidder breaking through the downed trees on the road beside the station.

Skidders are heavy machinery used in logging. With huge tires and massive, powerful bodies, they lift and transport downed trees from where they are cut to where logging trucks wait to be loaded to take them to the mill.

The big diesel engine and the cracking and crunching and scraping of trees out of its path is a welcome, beautiful sound.

As soon as the skidder creates an opening and moves out of the way, a large black truck pulls around from behind it over to us. At first I think maybe it's Ethan and Evan, but can see that, though similar, it's a different truck.

As Merrill climbs out of the driver's side, Anna climbs out of the passenger's door, and the girls squirm to get down and begin to shriek, Johanna yelling, "MOM. MOM. MOM." Taylor saying, "MOMMY. MOMMY."

I place them on the ground and they run to greet her.

As Anna sweeps them up into her arms and lavishes them with hugs and kisses, Merrill walks over and we embrace.

When we let go I can see that his eyes are glistening. "Wasn't sure I'd ever see y'all again," he says.

I nod. "Thank you so much for coming after us."

I see Carla climbing out of the backseat of the truck and rushing over to Anna and the girls.

"That was all Anna and Little Ben Trainer," he says. "She wasn't takin' *no* for an answer, so we followed him all the way down Overstreet after the storm. Took a while, but—"

"That's Ben Trainer?" I ask, nodding toward the large man climbing down from the skidder.

He nods.

"Why him?"

"Anna called Taunton's Timber and told them the situation and he volunteered. Why?"

"Doesn't matter," I say. "I'm just glad to see y'all."

Carla begins to scream. "NO. NO. PLEASE GOD NO. WHERE IS HE? WHERE? OH, GOD NO. JOHN PAUL. JOHN PAUL."

45

"How guilty do you feel?" Anna asks.

She, Merrill, and I are in the front seat of the truck he borrowed to come get us. Merrill is driving. Anna is in the middle.

Johanna and Taylor are lying in the back seat fast asleep, held fast by the three seatbelts wrapped around them.

"More than I can say."

We are on Overstreet, heading home, weaving our way around downed trees and debris on the path that Ben Trainer had cleared with the skidder on their way to get us.

The night is dark, none of its blackness broken up by street or house lights anywhere, the lone illumination the headlights of the truck shining weakly into the inky incomprehensible void.

North Florida is the land of slash pines no more. Based on what Anna and Merrill have told me and what I can see in the truck's headlights and the periphery spill from them, there are more trees down than standing— thousands of them, no, hundreds of thousands—broken, splintered, split open, fallen over in every direction. Though there's no question that the coastal areas are going to be the hardest hit—and probably nowhere more so than Mexico Beach—it's clear that Michael also did catastrophic damage a lot farther inland than any previous storm. The scope of the devastation is just dawning on me, and I wonder what shape we'll find Wewa in.

Though we told her there's nothing she can do and she'll be forced to leave as soon as more law enforcement backup or the National Guard arrives, Carla had insisted on staying in Mexico Beach.

"Would you leave if they were missing?" she had asked me, nodding toward the girls. "Think about what you just did to find them."

"I did that for John Paul too," I say.

"But you haven't found him yet. Why are you quitting?"

"I'm not," I say. "I'll be back in the morning with more

help. But there's nothing else we can do tonight. There's no electricity. It's dark and dangerous—"

"You wouldn't let danger stop you lookin' for them."

"I don't mean dangerous for me," I say. "I mean for John Paul or others out there. Do you realize how easy it would be to run over someone or bump into a pile of debris and crushing someone under or near it? Search and rescue operations will start tomorrow. Professionals who know what they're doing will be looking for him."

"Well, I can't leave," she had said, "and you shouldn't be able to either."

Ben Trainer had offered to remain behind and to use his skidder to clear the trees from any roads that the searches may need to get down at first light, but Merrill, Anna, and I had decided to get our girls back home, check on Dad and Verna, and for me to report in to Reggie and try and get another vehicle—something Carla said she would never forgive us for.

Anna takes my hand and squeezes it hard. "If there was anything else we could be doing tonight, we would," she says. "She lashed out at you because she feels responsible for them being out there in the storm in the first place. And she is—at least partially. Rudy shouldn't even have been at her place and she certainly shouldn't have gone to sleep and left the kids with him. She's trying her best to share the blame."

I nod.

Merrill says, "I got some things I'm gonna share with Rudy, we find his ass alive."

"Get in line," Anna says.

"If y'all could've seen Johanna holding onto Taylor in that upside-down shack with a dead body floating nearby during the middle of that storm with the house being ripped apart around them, you'd want to kill him with your bare hands—and take your time doing it."

"Already there," Anna says.

"My ass was as soon as I heard he took them," Merrill says.

Every few feet Merrill has to maneuver the large truck around logs and limbs and trees, their jagged edges scraping the sides of the vehicle, their pine needles and leaves brushing the bottom. The number, size, and species of trees is incalculable and seems infinite.

Anna begins to cry. "I'm so glad you found them. I can't imagine . . . If you hadn't . . . Thank you, John, for what you did."

"It's not hard to imagine what Carla is feeling, what she's going through," I say. "Because we just were."

"And given what you just did to find and save our girls . . ." Anna says. "It's easy to understand why she can't understand us leaving."

I nod and wonder what I would be doing right now if Johanna and Taylor were still missing, and ask myself why I'm not out there walking around searching with a flashlight for John Paul right now.

"I should've stayed," I say.

"I can turn this big bastard around," Merrill says.

"No way," Anna says. "No. We are taking our girls home and you're getting some rest and sleep and can begin searching for him and the hundreds others missing in the morning. Period. End of discussion."

Merrill says, "Mama done put her foot down."

"I thought I had lost all of you," she says. "I . . . I can't give you up just yet. It's only a few hours, there's nothing you could be doing down there anyway, and it's what I need right now."

I start to ask myself if she or I would be feeling or acting differently if Carla hadn't changed her mind and the adoption had gone through, but stop before I go too far down that dark path.

I would be out there looking if Johanna or Taylor were still missing, so why not John Paul? Is it because we didn't adopt him? Because I blame his mom and Rudy for what happened to my girls, for John Paul being missing? Or is it that I promised Johanna and Taylor that I wouldn't leave them tonight?

I let out a long, heavy sigh.

"We've got to turn around, don't we?" Anna says.

46

The disembodied sounds of the unseen sea as its waves roll in and gently crash against the storm-flattened shore and back out into the deep blackness again is hypnotic.

Merrill and I are in the truck, windows down, high beams on, slowly searching the ruins and remnants of Mexico Beach for little John Paul.

The truck, I learned, like the skidder and Little Ben Trainer, is a loaner from Taunton Timber.

"It's worse here," Merrill is saying, "but it's bad everywhere."

When we got back to the fire station I had awakened the girls and asked them if, since their mother was now with them, it was okay if they stay here with her and get some sleep while I went out searching for John Paul with

Uncle Merrill, assuring them I was willing to keep my promise not to leave them by letting them continue to sleep in the back of the truck while we drove around the desolate town.

They were only too happy for me to search for who they considered to be their little brother and are now sleeping on cots with Anna in the back of the station.

"More damage here no question," he's saying, "but you be hard pressed to find a home or business without at least some damage in Wewa—and I hear it's like that all the way to Marianna."

We have yet to see Carla. She, Ben Trainer, and Denny are also out here somewhere searching for John Paul.

Everywhere the headlights land, it looks as if a massive terrorist attack has happened, as if an excessive amount of explosives had been rigged to everything. Rubble. Wreckage. Ruin. Everywhere. Piles and piles and piles of two-by-fours and trusses and shingles and siding and furniture and carpet and appliances and clothes and vehicles and trees and limbs and beaches. Trucks and RVs on their sides or on top of other cars. Piles and piles of boats on top of each other in the marina—or slung ashore. Capsized. On their sides. With parts of their sides missing.

The devastation and destruction is so extensive and excessive it doesn't look real.

"You gonna need a new roof," he says. "And a fair bit of siding, but . . . 'sides that you good. We gonna need to get some tarps up there before it rains again."

Merrill's place in Pottersville is surrounded by downed trees but is otherwise okay.

"A lot of the places up our way look okay from the front," he is saying, "but because part of their roof got blown off, the wind and water damage has gutted the inside of their house. It's freaky. You can't tell it from the front. You think they good, then you go around back or inside and you see the front's just a facade."

I nod, then shake my head as I continue to scan the savaged landscape being illuminated by the truck's headlights for any sign of John Paul.

"Trees and trash everywhere," he says. "Most roads are completely blocked. Lots of people can't get out of their driveway because of them and some poor bastards can't get out of their houses 'cept by crawling out a window. And it's everywhere. Every street. Every house. Never seen anything like it. We went from quaint little towns to war-torn third world country in the course of a couple of hours. Everybody wanderin' around stunned, dazed, in shock, vacant, thousand-yard stare in their sad eyes. Can't communicate with the outside world—or each other, 'cept in person. Can't go anywhere. Cut off from any help. Supplies limited and dwindling fast. Shelters overrun. People who lost everything with no place to go, no way to get there, and couldn't get out even if there was."

It's hard to take in, to fathom that as bad as the storm was, the aftermath might be worse.

"I'm tellin' you . . ." he adds, "the recovery not gonna take months but years. And it'll never be the same again—not in our lifetime, maybe ever."

Earlier, when we had first seen each other, I had asked about his mom and fiancé, my dad and Verna, my brother, Reggie, and others—and though they're all alive, they are in the same condition and situation we're all in, waiting in the dark to see what tomorrow brings.

We reach the west end of town where a huge pile of fallen pines block the road, above which a small boat is some twenty feet up in a few of the bent but still standing trees, and he turns around.

"Got about a quarter tank left," he says. "Nowhere to get gas for at least fifty miles—maybe eighty. You want me to keep enough in here for us to get back to Wewa?"

I nod. "Think we should. Let's go look at the area around Rudy's car and Carl's house again. We can park it and search on foot."

On our way to the place where Carl's shack used to be, we passed hundreds of empty foundations, some of them with the tile flooring or hardwood laminate still partially visible beneath the sand and seaweed. Hundreds, maybe thousands, of entire houses gone, the only sign they were ever there are the foundations that couldn't hold them fast to the earth against the force of Michael.

When we pass the little strip mall shopping center that has been here since I was a kid, I can see that the storefronts of all the buildings are gone and in one of them, which was a kind of five-and-dime store when I was little and is now a restaurant, the back end of a black F-250 is sticking out of it. The camera mounts on it let me know that it's the twins.

"Pull over there for a minute," I say. "Need to have a quick word with Frick and Frack."

"They the ones cold-cocked you and took off?"

I nod.

He pulls into the parking lot and weaves around piles of plate glass, nail-studded boards, restaurant chairs and tables, beach accessories, and touristy T-shirts, and pulls directly behind them, his high beams making the surreal scene look like a night shoot on a movie set.

Ethan climbs out of the driver's side, holding his hand up to shield his eyes from the brights, and walks back toward us.

I jump out and head toward him, as Evan climbs out of the passenger side.

"I found my little girls a few minutes after you blind-sided me and took off," I say. "I could've used your help."

"John?" Ethan says. "I'm so sorry man. I've felt terrible

about that since . . . Really bad. I panicked. Thought we were gonna die if we didn't get away. Knew you weren't going to stop. I'm truly sorry. Please forgive me."

I can sense Merrill coming up behind me. Probably wants to make sure it's a fair fight if there's any trouble.

"Dude," Evan says. "It's okay. You're alive. We're alive. You found your girls. And we—we saved an old man and a fuckin' baby. A baby. Can't tell me that shit doesn't make up for everything else and then some."

47

"Thank you for what you did today," Anna whispers.

We are lying in our own bed again, Johanna and Taylor asleep on a bed we dragged in here for them.

The world outside our house has been flung into outer darkness. The world inside our home is just as black and lightless save for the small penlight on the dresser we're using for a nightlight for the girls.

"Our girls are alive because of you," she says.

"Johanna deserves far more credit for that than I do," I say. "What she did was . . ."

"Just incredible," she says. "I'm so proud of her."

We are lying with as little clothes on as possible on

top of the covers and are still hot, sweaty, sticky. Like the air outside, the air inside our home is still and humid, and there's nothing we can do about it.

"What you did saved John Paul's life too," she says. "If you hadn't abducted the twins they wouldn't have still been down there to rescue Rudy and him."

As the twins sped away from where they had left me to die, they nearly ran over an old man carrying a car seat with a baby in it. Swerving to avoid them, Ethan had crashed the truck into the open storefront restaurant. They had loaded up the old man and the baby and ridden the storm out there in the truck inside the restaurant. When the storm passed, Ethan and Evan had taken turns going out to look around but never saw anyone and so had decided to spend the night in the truck and hope help came in the morning. A large sign hanging down in front, the dark cave-like hole of the building, and the gray day and black night had obscured the truck, and no one passing by had seen it until Merrill and I rode by.

John Paul had been dehydrated and had a raging case of diaper rash, but was otherwise okay, and was reunited with his mother as soon as we could locate her.

And even though Rudy was in bad shape, I had punched him in the mouth when he tried to offer explanations and excuses for his actions, and warned him there was much worse awaiting him if ever came near me or my family again.

"Be real easy for you to still be a victim of this storm," Merrill had told him. "Lots of bodies gonna be found around here for the next week or so. Yours could be one of 'em. No one would ever know it was Hurricane Merrill and John instead of Michael."

Ever the victim, Rudy had skulked away as if he were the wronged and injured party.

"Did Carla's decision surprise you?" she asks.

We had offered for Carla and John Paul to come stay with us, but she had opted to stay at her place, saying it was time she grew up and started being responsible. I had figured her real reason for saying she would stay at her apartment was so Rudy could stay with her, but when he put in to sleep on her couch, saying it was just for tonight, which everyone knew it wouldn't be, she had given him a very firm *no* and had even told him that his only option was to ride the skidder back with Ben Trainer, who would drop him off at the shelter in Honeyville.

"A little," I say. "Yeah. I just hope it lasts. It's going to be hard. She's angry at him right now. She's upset, realizes how easily she could have lost her son because of him, but . . . that will fade eventually. It's what she does when it does that will be most telling."

"I hope she can retain her resolve," she says. "And really become the mother John Paul deserves."

I nod.

"Want me to stop talking so you can sleep?" she asks.

I let out a little laugh. "Never," I say, which I would have even if it wasn't too hot to sleep.

48

We wake to a new world.

A wet wasteland, the carnage of civilization littering the landscape in every direction.

No electricity.

No running water.

No phones.

No TV.

No local radio.

No grocery stores or gas stations.

No restaurants or auto parts places. Nothing essential or frivolous. Nothing existential. Nothing recreational.

No doctors. No hospitals.

Nothing.

And everyone has that same slightly stunned, thousand-yard stare of recently returned combat vets.

Everyone is at a loss. Everyone is overwhelmed. Everyone wonders where we even begin.

The innumerable downed trees alone—on houses and vehicles, blocking every driveway and street—is itself beyond daunting. Yet that is one minuscule aspect of our long, arduous road to recovery.

We are trapped in a fallen forest where we can't get in and out of our own driveways let alone down the street or out of town.

As if inmates in a type of collective solitary confinement, our unspoken sense of claustrophobia and anxiety hums beneath the surface, increasing, intensifying, influencing.

At first there was silence—a dazed, dumbfounded quietude that felt particularly deafening in the maddening blackness of our first lightless night—but now the new soundtrack of our storm-ravaged lives includes the near constant desultory sounds of chainsaws, generators, and the concerned and questioning conversations of people on their porches and in the streets because their homes no longer offer comfort or consolation.

Nearly all homes and businesses are damaged—many so catastrophically they're uninhabitable.

Most standing homes with nonstructural damage

have multiple families in them—refugees from wrecked and ruined homes of their own taken in by family and friends.

Among the leaning trees are leaning power poles. Among the downed trees are downed power poles. And weaving in and out of all the piles of trees and trash and all the debris-filled ditches, like Reynolds Woodcock's phantom thread, are thousands of miles of electric, phone, and cable lines.

Rumors spread like particularly pathological contagions, the void of information filled with misinformation, disinformation, and speculation.

Though those of us here have an experiential understanding of the storm and the havoc it has wreaked, it is those outside this dead zone, who have access to the reporting being done about the storm, that have the greater knowledge and understanding of the scope of the storm and the damage done.

The outside world is worried about us—some family and friends sick with it—but are unable to contact or communicate with anyone inside, and so are as blind and dumb as we are, only in a different way.

I am out in my front yard surveying the new reality of the post-apocalyptic landscape I now live in when Merrill pulls up in the big black F-250 Super Duty loaner from Taunton Timber and parks out on the road.

49

"Figured you'd be trying to get down to the sheriff's department," Merrill says.

We are winding our way around the branches and leaves and limbs that cover my yard and driveway as we move to meet each other somewhere between where he parked and where I was standing.

"I was just wondering how long it will be until 71 is clear," I say.

"Half the town's out there with their chainsaws," he says.

"I can hear them."

"Shouldn't be long until there's at least a one-lane path in every direction."

"Got no official vehicle and no desire to leave my girls," I say. "Besides, I'm stationed up here until further notice anyway. But I'll make my way down there eventually—check on Reggie. Need to check in with the prison, as well."

"Big parts of it blew away," he says. "Perimeter fences down, so inmates are on lockdown in the dorms. Can't even open the doors because of it. No staff can come in because of the trees blocking the roads, but even if they could they couldn't get in to relieve the staff that's there, because they can't open the damn doors for fear the inmates will rush them and escape. Since none of the grounds crews inmates can get out to work, a few of the officers on duty and some that live up there rounded up every chainsaw they could find and are cutting their way out even as people on this side are cutting their way in. Can you imagine how good the inmates are smelling—all trapped in the dorms with no electricity or running water. That's the real reason the COs deserve hazardous duty pay."

I shake my head. "Not to mention the mental and emotional state of the men in that stressful situation."

"Should've evacuated," he says.

"Even if we had known what the storm was going to become, there wouldn't've been time."

"Yeah."

Neither of us says anything for a moment, as we take it all in.

Eventually, he says, "Talked to Timbo—cousin of

mine works at the co-op. Says the main transmission lines coming into the county are down, so getting the poles and lines in town fixed ain't gonna do no good 'cause there's no power coming to them. Says it'd be like having your house perfectly wired but not having the electricity turned on yet. A head honcho from the power plant up in Alabama that supplies us here flew over the area in a helicopter, and he said not just the transmission lines but all the towers that hold them up are down too, and that we are, and I quote, *fucked*."

I frown and nod slowly, as I think about how to best get Anna and the girls to her parents' in Dothan.

"All the cell towers are down too. Ain't gonna be no quick fix for any of this shit."

I nod again.

"Only store open in town is Ace," he says. "Entire back of their building blew off, but Dawn Lister was up there before daybreak this morning letting people get what they need on credit. I'm talkin' 'bout the entire back half of the store—nothing but sky. Other places with less damage aren't open but she's up there standing in that wet, lanky store with a pen and a notepad writing down what people are getting, knowing some of them will never come back and pay. She's good people. Sure hope she not the one who killed Andrew."

I smile.

"She said for me to tell you to come up there when you can," he says. "Brad Price said to holla at him too when you can. We can take a ride up there now if you want."

50

Trees, power poles, cables, and lines have all been cut back just enough to clear a narrow path to pass through. In many places only one lane is open, and even then limbs and lines dangle overhead as branches and jagged tree bases rub against the rubber of the tires and scratch the doors and quarter panels of those venturing out.

Merrill and I make our way through our empty little town, slowly making a serpentine pattern around the debris and the fresh wood chips and sawdust accompanying each place where a felled tree has been cut to allow traffic through.

In the distance, on unseen side streets and down backwoods dirt roads, I hear the buzz of chainsaws, the groan of diesel engines, and the loud slapping hum of oversized knobby off-road tires rolling on pavement.

Because Wewa is a rural Southern town filled with farmers, loggers, and self-sufficient country folk who own their own chainsaws and large four-wheel-drive trucks and tractors—and who are only too happy to help their neighbors— I can guarantee the cleanup, recovery, and rebuild will go much quicker here than in other parts of the Panhandle.

The parking lot of Ace is packed and we have to actually drive past the store and park on the side of the highway.

As we get out and walk in, I look over at St. Lawrence, and wonder again who killed Andrew, why, and if I'll ever really know.

Inside, Ace is dim and dank, water standing on the floor, soggy items lining shelves, sheetrock and insulation hanging precariously from walls and ceilings.

And as Merrill had said, the entire back wall and a huge portion of the roof are gone, which on such a massive building is extremely disorienting.

Townspeople, tired, tattered, unkempt, and unwashed, stand in line clutching the items they most need at the moment as Dawn stands behind the counter writing them down in a composition book, using her phone as a calculator.

All through the warm, dusky store, stunned citizens

are searching for supplies, sharing stories, spreading rumors, offering condolences, and/or commiserating.

Long since out of chainsaws, generators, gas cans, and tarps, the store still has plenty to offer in the way of tools and nails and screws, Visqueen, lumber, plumbing pipe and fittings, and all manner of household and cleaning supplies. It's a haven for desperate people wanting to do something, to respond in some way to the full-on attack they've just suffered.

When Dawn sees us, she asks Levi if he'll take over for her for a moment and walks over to us.

I hug her and thank her for what she's doing for the town, and then apologize because I can tell both make her uncomfortable.

"Don't apologize," she says. "Not necessary. I'm just not a hugger and I embarrass easily—not to mention I'm sweaty, dirty, and smelly right now."

"You need help keepin' an eye on this place tonight," Merrill says, nodding toward the back, "you let me know."

"Thanks," she says. "I honestly don't think it'll be a problem. I hear a curfew will be in effect and I was gonna see if a deputy would drive by and check on it, but . . . Thank you."

"No problem."

She looks around and then waves us back to her office.

Inside her office, which is illuminated by the missing back wall, she says, "I had two things I wanted to talk to you about."

"Sure," I say.

"The first is . . . well, I know it's none of my business, but . . . I feel invested and I'm just worried that with the storm that maybe Andrew's killer might get away with it. I'd hate to see that happen and, well, I was just curious."

"Officially," I say, "all investigations have been suspended. We're operating in emergency mode right now and for the foreseeable future, but I'm still working the case as I can—and will until it's solved. No matter how long it takes."

"Oh, good. I'm real glad to hear that. If I can do anything to help, let me know."

"Thank you."

"The other thing was . . . well, I heard about what Johanna and Taylor and you went through . . . I just can't imagine what that was like—especially for them. Anyway, I put a generator back for y'all. Hopefully they can have a better night tonight with it. Let 'em have a little light and maybe even watch *Barney* or something. Anyway, use it as long as you need it—on the house—and I'll get it back from you when all this is over. I wish I had more gas to give you, but I'm afraid that's in shorter supply than generators."

Tears sting my eyes at this extraordinary act of kindness and I feel overwhelming joy and appreciation.

"I'm sorry," I say. "I know you're not a hugger, but I have to hug you again. Thank you so much. They will have a much better night. Everyone in town will because of you."

51

When we walk out into the parking lot, Reggie is pulling up in her official black sheriff's SUV.

I walk over to talk to her while Merrill pulls the truck around to the side of the building to have the generator loaded.

By the time I reach her vehicle, Reggie is getting out and we hug each other, lingering a little longer than we ever have before.

When we let go, she says, "They just cleared enough of 71 to get through and I had to come check on things here. Mom's place is completely flooded—all our stuff is ruined. Pictures. Everything. Only clothes I own are the ones I'm wearing right now. Mom and the kids are staying with a friend of ours in Orlando and I have no way to let them know I'm even alive."

Like so many people I've encountered since the storm, her eyes are moist.

"Oh, Reggie, I'm so sorry to hear that. Please stay with us."

"Honestly, I'll be staying at the sheriff's department for the foreseeable future."

"Well," I say, "when you're not . . ."

"Wasn't sure I was ever going to see you again," she says. "Or your little girls. I truly didn't know."

I nod. "It's so good to be here, to be alive, and to see you. How are you?"

She lets out a harsh little laugh and shakes her head. "Overwhelmed. Ill-prepared. Strung out. Sleep-deprived. Heartbroken. In shock. Traumatized. Glad to still be here but not sure exactly where here is anymore, or how to be its sheriff."

I nod. "You'll figure it out. This county's lucky to have you."

"Did you happen to talk to Merrick before the storm came in?" I ask.

She nods.

Merrick McKnight, our friend and her ex-boyfriend, moved to Panama City to work as a reporter about six months ago.

"He sent his kids to Tampa, but he stayed. Think he

was actually in the News Herald building when it hit. That was his plan, anyway. I hope he's okay."

"The damage is . . . All the way back to the post office it looked like the buildings were in St. Joe Bay, like one of those abandoned towns they're flooding for a new lake—but it wasn't abandoned. We were all still there. You know firsthand how Mexico Beach is—nearly completely demolished . . . but I bet you well over seventy-five percent of the homes and businesses in Gulf County are damaged—many of them beyond repair. And now we got no supplies—no food, no water, no gas, no stores open. There's no electricity on anywhere. No phone service. Our radios are out. Hell, virtually all the towers in the county are down. Our whole county is now like a war zone. It's like bombs have gone off everywhere. Or like the fuckin' apocalypse happened and we're the only survivors. We're completely isolated from the outside world."

I think about the reality of what she's describing and how accurate it really is.

"We're gonna have far more deaths than we planned for," she says. "I can't imagine how many in Mexico Beach alone."

The majority of Mexico Beach is in Bay County. As the sheriff of Gulf County, Reggie won't have to deal with them. She's mentioning the fatalities as a citizen, a human being, not as a sheriff.

"Anyway . . ." she says, "I've got to get back to the station."

"What can I do?" I ask. "What do you want me doing?"

"Help out up here," she says. "Keep order, give aid, do what you can. We're instituting a curfew starting tonight. Help enforce that. Within another day or so backup will arrive. We'll have all types of emergency services— FEMA, Red Cross, Samaritan's Purse, Cajun Navy, and other agencies from around the state will send us officers to assist us. Then hopefully we can start getting supplies in here so we can survive."

"What did you do with the van?" I ask.

"The van?"

"The stolen one with the burned body in it in Dalkeith," I say.

"Oh. Wow. Yeah. Left it where it was. Had no other option at the time. That old barn in front of it is now on top of it, so . . . we're fucked from an evidentiary aspect."

I tell her about seeing the men from the van in the hurricane house during the storm. "I let our guys and the Bay County deputies know about it while I was down there. The house is on the Bay County side."

"Probably thought they were going to do some serious looting during the storm," she says. "No matter what they did, they'll probably get away with it. I hate it, but probably be a lot of crimes committed during this time that we can't do anything about—not until we get some backup and communications and can get out of survival mode. Even then . . . all our investigators are having to act as deputies. And given the state of things . . . we're gonna have more stress-related crimes. More domestic violence. More assaults. Hell, everyone is walking around with PTSD. Like I said, I hate it and we don't want to advertise the fact, but . . . them are the facts. We can only do the barest survival mode basics right now."

I'm well aware of the reality she's so accurate describing, but I'm not about to let go of any case or give anyone a pass—not Andrew's killer, not criminals who come into our county during a state of emergency to rape and plunder and pillage while we're at our most vulnerable.

"Well, as soon as I can, I want to look into it—and to get back to investigating Andrew's murder."

She laughs. "As if you ever stopped. I'm not saying we're gonna let anything go or that we're not gonna try our damnedest to investigate and clear every case, but . . . the reality is . . . Look at our reality right now. Let's survive first . . . Then, if we do that, we'll try to catch some bad guys."

52

For the rest of the day, I assisted the deputies on duty in and around Wewa.

There wasn't much we could do. We had no resources and no real answers to the questions we were asked, but we were present and visible, calming and reassuring.

In the late afternoon, Merrill returned from a supply run, and he and I are now on my steep roof tacking down bright blue tarps over the places where the shingles and siding are missing.

I'm not sure when I'll be able to have my roof repaired, and I don't want to have to worry about more damage occurring while I'm concentrating on other things over the next few weeks—like surviving, assisting my neighbors, and finding Andrew's killer.

"Damage goes way up," he says. "Never seen anything like it. Every tree eighty miles up is down or leaning. Had to go all the way to Dothan to find any supplies—and they're running low. They's a shit ton of evacuees up there."

The three large oak trees in my front yard look bare and bald, many of their limbs and branches and nearly all their leaves covering the driveway and the yard beneath them.

"Thank you for going."

"Got shit else to do. Wish I could've gotten more."

Our old house is two stories and the pitch of the roof is extreme, but the view from up here in the early evening is breathtaking and provides some perspective on the savaged world below. Lake Julia is calm, the smooth surface of her dark face like slate. Many of the cypress trees that used to border her edges are now lying partially submerged along the rim of her soggy shallow banks.

"How is Dothan?" I ask.

"They got a little damage, but mostly it's just crowded," he says. "Got electricity and running water. Parts of it are untouched."

"I'd really like for Anna and the girls and whoever else wants to to go to her folks up there—maybe tomorrow."

"Be a good place for 'em," he says. "I can make another run for supplies—gather up more gas cans and a list of what we need—and take them or they follow me and I can make sure they get there."

"Ah man, thank you so much. That would be awesome."

The generator Dawn secured for us is running in the side yard, the reverberation of its loud, incessant go-cart-like engine ricocheting off my neighbors' house and bouncing up here. It is powering our refrigerator right now and a fan for the girls to read and play in front of. It joins the myriad other generators and chainsaws that can't be seen but are heard echoing throughout our little torn-up town.

"Caught a little news coverage while I was up there," he says. "Talked to some people from other places. Was a motherfucker of a storm. Panama City Beach is okay, but Panama City got hit hard. Worse than us, not quite as bad as Mexico Beach. Say it wiped out Tyndall."

Tyndall is the Air Force Base in between Panama City and Mexico Beach and is the training facility of the F-22 Raptor, the most advanced and most expensive stealth tactical fighter in the world.

"Say they lost several of the F-22 Raptors," he says. "That's a few hundred million a pop."

I shake my head and drive in another tack.

"Panama City is about like us—everything damaged. No electricity. No water. No supplies. I'm tellin' you . . . we all fucked."

"Were you able to get through to Susan?"

Susan is my ex-wife and Johanna's mother, and I had asked Merrill to call her and let her know that Johanna is alive and well as soon as he got cell service.

"Left her a message, but then she called me back. Told her y'all all good. Didn't mention Rudy or Mexico Beach or anything. Told her the plan was to still get the girls to Anna's parents' place in Dothan and y'all call her once she was there."

"Thanks. How'd she sound?"

"Like she always do when talkin' to me—coldly civil. Carefully polite. But she's glad to get the info. Even said *thank you*. What gonna happen when she find out her little girl rode out the storm out in it at ground zero?"

"Whatever it is it'll be a Category 5. And who can blame her? She'll probably fight for full custody again and this time she might get it."

"You pressing kidnapping charges on Rudy?" he asks.

"I damn sure am. Reckless endangerment and some others too."

"Good. He's gettin' off far lighter than he should."

"Yes, he is," I say, and aggressively drive in another tack.

When we finish the roof, Merrill and I grill the meat from our freezer that has thawed on the back patio, as the sun sets beyond leaning and limbless trees on the far side of Julia.

We are joined for dinner and the night by Dad, Verna, Jake, Carla, John Paul, Za, and an elderly neighbor who doesn't need to be alone.

Then, in a hot house even with the windows open, we gather around our table beneath a light powered by the generator Dawn provided us and eat meat without side dishes and drink room temperature bottled water and are grateful for all of it—the company, the light, the food and drink, the safety, and the shelter.

We make pallets on the living room floor and all sleep in there between box fans that can't drown the sound of generators coming from the open windows.

The next morning, Za returns to the hospital, Merrill leads a caravan of Anna and the girls, Verna, Carla, John Paul, and our elderly neighbor to Dothan, and I venture back out into my nearly unrecognizable hometown to offer assistance, comfort, order, safety, and to search for Andrew Irwin's killer.

53

W ith most of the main highways and roads at least partially open, people begin to pour into the area.

Our little town has never had so much traffic—not even during peak tourist season. Most of it just passes through on its way to Port St. Joe and Mexico Beach, but some stays here—or returns here after realizing Mexico Beach is still closed while search and rescue takes place. The rumor circulating, which is not an untruth so much as an exaggeration, is that hundreds of bodies have been found and that the medical examiner's office has run out of body bags.

Help comes in the form of official, humanitarian, religious, and capitalistic.

Officials from the federal and state levels arrive in

long lines of black SUVs escorted by highway patrol cars, lights flashing, their convoys moving faster than anyone else on the road.

The Red Cross and Samaritan's Purse and other random humanitarian and religious organizations arrive with supplies—mostly bottled water, MREs, and tarps.

With the help of disaster relief volunteers, residents begin to blue roof the town.

Individuals, couples, families, church groups show up with pickups pulling trailers with diapers and baby wipes, food, water, and cleaning supplies. Some of these same individuals and groups or others like them show up with boxes of hamburgers and hotdogs and buns and gas grills, and set up on the green in front of Lake Alice Park in the middle of town and cook and give out free food until their supplies give out. Several of these Good Samaritans share how they had lived through a hurricane before and had survived on the kindness of strangers and were only paying forward the debt they can make payments on but never pay off.

Among these brilliant examples of compassion and humanity there are also conmen and hucksters getting paid in advance for work they never intend to do or collecting the personal information of desperate, gullible people they convince they represent FEMA or some other governmental or insurance agency.

But these are rare, and what the opened roads bring in mostly represents the very best of humanity.

All these people. All these vehicles. All this energy and activity.

And yet—post-hurricane time is slow time.

For most people there is nowhere to go and no way to get there. There are none of the distractions that phones and internet and TV provide.

And in what feels like August heat with no air-conditioning and no running water, time moves languidly along like the slow trickle of a bead of sweat snaking down a sun-baked back.

As I slowly make my way through the elongated day, helping and assisting and giving aid where I can, I think about who could have killed Andrew and why. I'm curious about the body in the stolen van and the men in the hurricane house, and hope to get to them eventually, but for now it is the seemingly motiveless murder of a good and innocent man that sits at the center of my obsession, that has captured the full attention of my imagination and won't let go.

I think through the witness statements and try to suss out the half-truths and the lies and the motives behind them.

And with no clear motive, I turn the spotlight of my focus onto means and opportunity. If I can't figure out why someone would kill Andrew, then perhaps my best hope of catching the killer is to determine who had the access that would enable them to do it.

Who had access to Andrew's life, to his refrigerator—when he was home and when he wasn't?

That leads me to wonder who, if anyone, had a key to St. Lawrence.

Who could've waited until Andrew was out walking Mary and slipped in and swapped his orange juice container for the poisoned one? Of course, to do it, the killer had to know what kind of juice Andrew drank ahead of time, which means he or she had to be pretty familiar with Andrew and his habits.

I believe Peggy Munn had said she had a key, and she was certainly familiar with the juice he drank—she actually bought it for him sometimes. Did anyone else have a key? Did anyone else know him that well? Of course, after deciding to kill him the killer could have made it her or his business to know his schedule and habits and what kind of orange juice he drank. What about Jan Epps? Did she have a key back when she was active in the church and acted like it was hers? Did she keep it? What about Levi? Did Andrew offer him something to drink during one of his visits or tell him to help himself to what was in the fridge? And why was he visiting?

As I drive the truck Dad let me borrow back toward the church that became Andrew's home, I pull out my phone to call Melissa Epps, forgetting it has no service.

I decide to drive around to see if I can get through to the Epps's place so I can ask her, but when I get close to Ace I see Levi loading some PVC into a customer's truck in the parking lot and pull in.

Rolling down my window, I motion him over when he finishes loading the joints of pipe.

"We're slammed," he says. "I gotta get back inside to help Miss Dawn."

"Won't take but a minute," I say. "We have witnesses that say you went over to visit Father Andrew sometimes. I was just wondering why. What'd y'all do? What'd you talk about?"

"Just God and shit," he says. "I'm an atheist. Or thought I was. Always thought religion was bullshit for the weak-minded."

"But?" I ask.

"But . . . I don't know. Just been wonderin' about morality, right and wrong, the afterlife, shit like that. I been questioning some of the things I do, some of the— of what I believe. And I'd been having these dreams. I was gonna talk to him about it, about all of it—even thought I might do a confession or whatever with him, but I . . . never . . . talked to him about any of it really before he died. Was working up my nerve but . . . then he got killed."

"Did you ever eat or drink anything while you were there?"

"At the church—or his house or whatever it is —no. Why?"

"Anyone ever come over while you were there?"

"I really gotta go," he says. "I think one time that meth mom from across the street came over and maybe that Madison chick from next door. I don't know, man. But I gotta get back to work. Okay?"

"Okay. Thanks for talking to me."

When I pull out of Ace, I decide instead of driving around to the Epps's to pull into St. Lawrence and park there and walk back as far as I can into the woods to see if Melissa might be out there.

But when I walk around to the back I can see that the storm blew so much of the woods down that they're impassable, that there's no longer a path between the two properties.

When I walk back around to the front I see Tad and Madison and their boys out in their yard picking up limbs and raking leaves, and walk over.

"That was some blow, wasn't it?" Tad says as I reach them.

"Yes it was."

They both stop working, him leaning, and give me their undivided attention.

Like so many of the houses around town theirs has already been blue roofed.

"We're luckier than most," he says. "No structure

damage. Nothing bad happened to any of us. We're alive and together and only have a little damage."

"How'd your place do?" Madison asks me.

"Same," I say. "Minor damage comparatively. I know y'all are busy so I won't keep you. I just wondered if either of you ever saw anyone let themselves into Andrew's— like with their own key, whether he was there or not?"

Tad shakes his head. "No, I never did. Did you?" he asks his her.

"Can't swear to it," Maddy says. "But seems like I've seen that rich lady from behind the woods back there go in a time or two. Now that you say it. . . Seems like both times were when Andrew wasn't home, but I can't swear to any of that. I wouldn't even say it if it was anyone else, but she is such a bitch."

54

Each new day brings more people in, most of whom leave again by sundown—because of the curfew and because there is nowhere to stay.

Work crews with camper trailers are desperately looking for places to park them with hookups, but nearly all the campgrounds and trailer parks in the area have been destroyed. Some of them are driving from Tallahassee or Panama City Beach each day, adding about four hours of commuting to their long, strenuous, dangerous day's work.

The lines of traffic in both directions on Highway 71 seem to stretch all the way from Blountstown to the bay —service vans, pickup trucks loaded down with workers pulling trailers loaded down with tools and materials, semis, supplies, and cars filled with evacuees returning to see if they have a place to return to, and if so, what shape it's in.

And all of this with no electricity, no phones or communications of any kind, and no running water.

Everyone is hot and sticky and smelly and miserable, and yet kindness, patience, and neighborly concern mostly abounds. Locals help each other and share what they have and big-hearted strangers keep pulling into town with food, water, and supplies.

So many donations pour into our little town, in fact, that we decide we need a central receiving and distribution center, and unfortunately the place chosen is the old gym on Main Street where Merrill and I used to play a few times a week. Soon it is completely filled with clothes and blankets and diapers and tampons and canned food and bottled water and bleach and dog food and wipes and toilet paper and paper towels and tarps and MREs. Volunteers, mostly from Glad Tidings Assembly of God, mostly teens from their youth group under the guidance of Taylor and Meleah Smith, unload trucks in the back and pass out boxes of supplies in the front to residents who pull through in their cars and pop their trunks.

As sad as it makes me to think that it will be weeks or months before we can play basketball again, it is truly inspiring to see the sheer volume of donations and the tireless efforts of the volunteers to get them to those who most need them.

Law enforcement arrives in droves. Suddenly, sheriff deputies' cars from other counties in Florida are on every corner, patrolling every street, many of them in full tactical gear—this along with the curfew and the Third World conditions makes our town seem in some ways like a police state.

Now joining the sounds of chainsaws and generators and diesel engines and knobby tires rolling down the roads are the shrill squeals and harsh abrupt blurts of sirens—which can be heard both in the distance and in close proximately to where you are. No matter where you are.

The Marion County Sheriff's Department provides its chopper and aviation officer to Reggie, which not only allows her to get to places quickly when she needs to but enables her to send him on important supply runs to Tallahassee in about a quarter of the time it would take to drive.

Though the Verizon towers are all down and most people in the area have Verizon phones because the signal has always been much stronger here, we discover that both AT&T and Sprint cell phones work in certain limited capacities in some limited places.

The primary place the phones work somewhat is on bridges, so at any time throughout the day residents can be seen standing on the few bridges in the county trying to communicate with the outside world.

After discovering this, Reggie sent the Marion County chopper to Tallahassee for some eighty AT&T phones, only to discover when they were brought back that in order to work they had to have been activated here prior to the storm. We did, however, find a few burner phones confiscated in drug busts in the evidence locker that worked, so a few on the force could talk to each other.

With Anna and the girls and Carla and John Paul safe and well in Dothan, I live like a bachelor, coming and going as I please, working nonstop, and with no family or curfew to keep me in at night, I help and assist deputies during the day and work Andrew's case at night.

I, like everyone else in the region, am living a strange new reality in a strange new world, adapting as best I can to the surreal circumstances I suddenly find myself in.

By the Saturday following the storm, Verizon had trucked in portable cell towers that provided weak, spotty, temporary service within a few miles of the towers, which were placed in all three towns—Wewa, Port St. Joe, and Mexico Beach. The moment the towers went live all over town you could hear the bleeps and dings and vibrations of notifications from four days of missed calls and messages from worried family members and friends.

One of my first messages is from the other end of the continent—Harry Bosch, an LAPD detective, mentor, and friend, checking on me and letting me know that he had raised some funds to help me and the people in the area in need, and that it had already been wired to me. And not for the first time during this ordeal my eyes stung and I had to blink several times and swallow hard to get the lump out of my throat.

So much of the best of humanity on display, kind, generous, caring people doing what they can, giving what they can, offering what they can—comfort, compassion, sustenance—and I think again about how Andrew would be right in the middle of it all doing all he could for his neighbors, former parishioners, and friends, and it made me even more frustrated that I wasn't getting anywhere with his case.

55

With Ake's Septic Service using its trucks to pump out the lift station's lines, the city is able to turn on the water for a few hours each day, so that we can grab a cold shower and refill our tubs so we can wash our hands and flush our toilets when the water is not on.

Of course, you have to be at home during the short window in which it is turned on, and if you're not you have to make sure you didn't leave any taps open or faucets on or you'll come home to a house whose flood is only collaterally related to the storm.

As hot and sweaty as we all are you'd think a cold shower would feel good—and eventually it does, but even in our overheated and sticky state it has to be eased into.

It's amazing the difference being able to shower makes. I feel more awake, more alert, sharper, fresher—better mentally and emotionally as much physically.

As I help patrol the town, I use my spotty, limited cell service to call Melissa Epps, who I haven't been able to locate in the past few days.

"New phone, who dis?" she says, with street affect.

"John Jordan."

"Oh, hey, John Jordan," she says, her voice becoming friendly and tinged a bit with a playful edge. "Phone keeps blowin' up since it came back on."

"How are you?" I ask. "How'd y'all do during the storm?"

She tells me in detail how they did and that they are physically fine. "Jan is more of a cunt than ever, but . . . I don't think she and Dad will be together much longer. Thank Christ. Hey, speaking of havin' my phone blown the fuck up . . . people been callin' me to see if I've been arrested yet. Say they heard I killed Father Andrew. You been tellin' them that?"

"Of course not," I say. "I don't talk to the public about cases I'm working. Who has been—"

"But do you think I did it?"

"Right now I have no idea who did it or why," I say. "Did you?"

"Why would I?"

"Why would anyone?" I say.

"If I did . . ." she says, "and I didn't confess and no one helped me so they couldn't like turn on me or whatever . . . Do you think I could get away with it?"

"There's always physical evidence," I say. "And even circumstantial evidence. There are a lot of ways to make a case."

"But . . . getting a jury to buy it . . . That's another matter, isn't it?"

"I hear you and Father Andrew had a little book club," I say.

"Yeah, we got into a heated argument over Jane Austen and I killed him," she says. "I was all like, don't talk Brontës to me, bitch, and then slit his throat. Anything else?"

"Do you or your family have a key to St. Lawrence?"

"Huh?" she says. "You're breaking up."

"Do y'all have a key to St. Lawrence?"

"Oh," she says. "No."

"I thought your—ah, Jan, might have one from back when she was active there."

The phone cuts off and I can't tell if the call was dropped or if Melissa hung up on me, but when I try to call her back it goes straight to voicemail. I try her a few more times but each time the same thing happens.

As I pass Lake Alice Park, I see a man and a woman

with a folding table and a grill making hamburgers for people, and there in the line, towering over everyone else, is Little Ben Trainer.

I pull over and park, then get out and cross the street over to where he is.

"Can you believe this?" he says, nodding toward the middle-aged couple cooking and serving. "Came up from Hollywood, Florida just to feed people here. I'm sure people around here wouldn't mind if a cop skipped in line."

"No, thanks," I say. "I've already eaten. I just wanted to thank you again for bringing my wife to me and our girls the night of the storm."

"Ah, I's happy to do it. Glad Carla Jean found her little 'un too. Didn't think we were going to there for minute. She's awful tore up about it."

While the man flips the burgers on the grill, the woman stands at the table, laying out buns on plates and then adding potato chips and small condiment packages, both of them sweating profusely beneath their big sun hats.

"Can you believe how fuckin' hot it is in October?" Ben says. "And with no damn AC neither. I . . . Near 'bout the only place I'm the least bit cool is in my truck. Tempted to sleep in it at night but figure I'll die of carbon monoxide poisoning. Besides, gas is damn hard to come by."

"Yes, it is," I say.

"Though I hear the IGA and Dixie Dandy are gettin' generators so they can run their pumps a few hours a day."

I nod. And look around. Most people take their hamburgers to go but a few have taken them over to the park and are sitting beneath the main pavilion eating. The park and the lake behind it are still peaceful and picturesque, but downed oak trees and at least one smashed pavilion litter the tableau.

"You ever find out who killed that old priest?" Ben asks.

"Gettin' close," I say.

"Sure hope you don't think me or my mom has anything to do with it," he says. "She's had her issues with . . . you know, staying clean, but she wouldn't hurt anyone under any situation and I wouldn't kill nobody over a damn dog—no matter how much I liked it. Might kill their dog . . . But I wouldn't kill them. Just wouldn't."

"Did you ever see anyone let themselves into his place?" I ask. "Into the old church."

He looks up and squints. "Yeah. Seems like someone was always going in there—mostly women, but yeah."

"Any idea who?"

"You mean that just used a key and let themselves in?" he says. "Miss Munn was always doing it. That Jan Epps bitch too. And her crazy stepdaughter, I think. Other people visited but I think those are the only ones who didn't have to knock and wait to be let in. Oh, wait. There was one guy who let himself in too. Don't know his name but he's young and always has a red Ace shirt on."

Dear Diary,

I'm pretty sure I got away with it.

I thought I would, but you never know until you know, right?

I think I would have anyway, but we had the storm of the century here, and everything is fucked. I mean really fucked. Everyone is in survival mode now. There is no electricity, no running water, and no communications of any kind. The cops are busy with this shit. They're not even looking for me anymore.

It makes me wonder . . . Did God or the universe send the storm to make sure I got away with it? Or is everything random, coincidental, haphazard, chaotic? It's interesting to think about—when I can. My mind is still not working right. I guess it never will again. But when I'm semi-lucid like now it really trips me out to think about. Is there any rhyme or reason to anything?

Was I inspired to do what I did by God and then he sent the storm to make sure I got away with it? Who the hell knows? How can I know? Drive me crazy to think about it. I think and think and think and get a bad headache and throw up.

The headaches are getting worse.

My mind is my enemy.

Sometimes I forget what I'm

I don't think I'll kill again. I did my experiment. Saw what I saw. But I didn't really enjoy it. Really didn't do anything for me. It was what it was. But nothing about it made me want to do it again.

Think I'm about to lose my fucking job. So there's that. Fuck! I hate my fucking head sometimes. Why can't I ever get one moment of fucking peace?

What was I

Think I lost my train

Just nod and smile. Be pleasant and polite and no one will ever know. No one will suspect anything.

I don't care if they do. I really don't. I'm sick of all this shit. I really am. Just want it to stop. Make

Make it stop. Make it stop. Make it stop. STOP. STOP. Shut the fuck up. Please. Please stop. Just for a minute. Stop hurting. Stop screaming. Stop tormenting me. Please, for fuck sake!

56

When I arrive at Ace, Levi Tucker is helping Brad Price load a generator into his truck.

When they finish, Brad and I hug.

"Heard what happened," he says. "So glad you and my little ice cream-eating buddies are okay."

"Thanks. It was . . ."

"Rudy needs to be strung up," he says.

"May call you for help if it comes to that."

"Do," he says. "Be happy to help."

"How'd you fare during the storm?" I ask.

"Trees down or halfway down," he says. "Shingles. Little roof damage, but . . . I'm lucky compared to most."

"Looks like you're going to have some electricity tonight," I say, nodding toward the generator in the back of his truck.

He looks at me with tears in his eyes. "A man who's out of the country right now—over in India or Africa or somewhere—called and bought this for me. Said give it to a first responder hero and they gave it to me."

That brought tears to my eyes. And I realize again how tender we all are since the trauma of the storm—especially to seeing a friend or loved one for the first time and to acts of kindness, especially those by strangers.

"I'm so glad, man," I say. "You are a hero and you do deserve it. Hey, Anna and the girls are at her folks in Dothan. I'm gonna be grilling the last of the meat from our freezer tonight and it happens to be steaks. I think Merrill and Jake and maybe Reggie are coming over. Swing by and eat with us if you can."

"I'll do that," he says. "Steak sounds mighty good."

As we've been talking, Levi has been lingering a few feet away. When Brad pulls off, he steps up and says, "You here to see me?"

"Do you or did you have a key to Andrew's place?" I ask.

"*What*? No. No way, man. And this is harassment. I know my constitutional rights. You can't just keep harassing me like this."

"It's just I have a witness who says they saw you let yourself in."

"*Let myself in*?" he says. "As in opened the door for myself? Sure. I done that. I'd call to see if he had a minute to talk and he'd say come on over and come on in. I'll be waiting for you. So yeah, I opened the goddamn door for myself but I didn't have no key. Now, I'm done talkin' to you. You want to know anything else, talk to my lawyer."

I smile. "You have a lawyer, Levi? Cause the only way that works is if you actually have a lawyer."

"Well, no, I guess I don't, but I'm still done talkin' to you. So . . ."

"Well, hey," I say, "it was fun while it lasted."

"You laugh at me and I'll kick your ass," he says.

Before I realize what I'm doing, I step toward him, bringing my face to within inches of his. "Levi, let me tell you something. I'm not a skinny, insecure teenage girl with low self-esteem, so you might want to think long and hard before you do anything like that or even threaten it. But in case you're serious, just know that I am laughing at you right now. I'm laughing my ass off at you and I'm begging for you to beat my ass. Please. The first shot is free. Make it a good one. Come on."

"You've got a fuckin' gun, man," he says. "I'm not gonna—"

"I swear to you I won't draw it—not under any circumstance," I say.

"Man, fuck you," he says, and turns to walk away.

And I stand there realizing what an idiot I am and hoping my impulsive, ego-stoked stupidity isn't something he'll take out on Auburn tonight.

57

Leaving Dad's truck parked at Ace, I walk down the shoulder of Highway 71 to St. Lawrence, like Andrew and Mary had done so many times, and let myself in.

Inside the dark building, I make my way to the sanctuary and take a seat on one of the pews.

Calming down and saying a prayer of protection for Auburn, I realize how much less time I spend in sanctuaries these days.

As I have transitioned into part-time chaplaincy, I have become less of a chaplain at the same time I have become more of a cop, and while I find the work I'm doing immensely fulfilling, I miss not doing chaplaincy as much, not spending as much time in sanctuaries.

I recall reading something Frederick Buechner wrote

about being a part-time novelist and a part-time Christian and wondering if either were doing much of anyone any good.

Should I be doing more chaplaincy and less detecting? Should I be doing something else entirely? How can I use the modest gifts and skills I have to be of most benefit to those around me?

Sitting here I wonder if Andrew missed being a priest, if sitting here in this sanctuary, living here in this former church made him feel like one or miss it more.

Looking around I think about the life Andrew had here. Was he happy? Fulfilled? Was the platonic love of Peggy enough for him or is she lying about that and they had more? Did her husband wonder the same thing and kill him?

As my eyes wander about the dim sanctuary they come to rest on the old wooden confessional, and I am drawn to it.

Standing up from the pew, I make my way over to it, running my hand along the hard wood edges, wishing Andrew was here to hear my confession, wondering who heard his.

It's when I draw the curtain open on the penitent's side of the confessional that I see it.

Why didn't I think of looking in here sooner?

It had been searched initially, but I haven't look in it

since then, which is when the killer would have come back and left it.

Reaching into my pocket I pull out a pair of latex gloves, put them on, then pull out my phone.

Tapping in my passcode because my thumbprints can't be read through the gloves, I tap on the flashlight and take a good look at it.

A rush of adrenaline surges through my body and my heart rate quickens.

Opening my camera app and turning on the flash, I take several pictures of it before carefully lifting it.

It is a printed confession on white printer paper and as I begin to read it I know immediately it's from the actual killer.

My Confession

I KILLED ANDREW IRWIN. Or Father Andrew if you prefer. Makes no never mind to me. It's funny, I don't feel any guilt or remorse and yet the act of writing this down, of stating that I'm the one who did it so directly is creating a sensation in me I find hard to describe. I definitely feel lighter somehow. Not unburdened exactly, because I haven't been burdened, but I do feel something. I can't imagine what saying it out loud to someone would do—and that's not something I'll ever experience. I have no desire to confess, to be judged for what

I've done, to be arrested or put on trial or possibly put in prison.

I just wanted to say I did it. It was me. No one will ever know but me, so I wanted to write it down, not really to explain myself but maybe to sort of explain myself.

The thing is, and this is the absolute truth, I just decided to kill someone. To see if I could do it. To know what it would be like. To see if I could do it and not get caught. That's it, really. No big deal. Just sort of like an experiment I guess.

I'm not sure when exactly I first had the formalized thought, but it seemed to have been there for a while and while I was vaguely aware of it, at some point I just became like really aware of it.

And this is the kicker. I didn't realize it at the time, didn't put this very obvious thing in context. Can't believe I didn't. But it didn't take me too long to see it. But it's just interesting to me that I didn't see the direct link between them. Anyway, the thing is, I had been reading Crime and Punishment when I got the idea. Well, listening to the audiobook, which I feel like is reading, though I know some people don't. I guess actually I had finished the book by the time I became aware of the thought, so I'm not sure if it first formed while I was reading or shortly after and it doesn't matter but it had to start while I was reading it I think. It had to, right? How could it not. But anyway, I didn't become aware of the thought until well after I had finished the book, which is probably why I didn't connect them at first, but even still I'm embarrassed that I didn't see the connection. *But like I said the thought was fully formed just sort of hanging there when I became aware of it, so it had to have been there for a while and I think it must have at least had its seed in the reading, or listening to, of that great and terrible book.*

All that's sort of beside the point, but I find it interesting.

So here's my confession. I decided I wanted to kill somebody. Just like that. Just that simple and straightforward. I wanted to try it, to take someone's life. But whose?

I thought about it for a while. I thought about maybe killing a pedophile or a wife beater or a crook or something but decided I wanted it to be more random than that. This wasn't punishment. I'm not a cop. This is an experiment. This is just a thing I want to do. And to do it as some sort of retribution or payback or vigilante bullshit would change it.

So I wanted to kill some random, but who?

I wanted to find someone with little or no connection to me but who was on their own so I wouldn't accidentally kill someone else or more than one person. So I began looking around and I came upon Andrew. He lives alone. He has no connection to me. And while it occurred to me that he was old and sort of sad and lonely, that really didn't factor in, but I did realize that he had already lived most of his life and that he wasn't having much of a life anyway.

So eeny meeny miny moe and Andrew . . . is . . . it. That's all there was to it. Nothing more. Nothing less. No hidden sin he's being punished for—at least none that I know of.

They say motiveless murders are the most difficult to solve and get a conviction for, so that's what I did.

Even still I knew I was taking a risk. I could fuck up in some way I didn't even know about and get caught, but now I really don't think that's going to happen, especially with the storm. I don't think the cops are even investigating it anymore. Hell, how could they be? They're in survival mode just like the rest of us. So, thank you, Michael, for the extra insurance.

You may be wondering how it felt to do it, to kill someone. Well, maybe I'm a sociopath, I probably am, but it didn't feel like much of anything really. To be honest I was hoping for more. I thought it might be orgasmic or something but it wasn't much more than removing an opponent's bishop off a chess board. Maybe if he had been a bishop . . . but he was just a lowly old ex-priest.

Whoever reads this or if it gets turned over to the authorities is probably wondering if I plan to ever do it again. Well . . . ever is a long time, but right now I have no plan or desire to ever do it again. That could change but at this point I don't see it doing so. I wanted to do it. I did it. It was what it was and now I'll move on to something else. What that is exactly I don't know, but stay tuned. I'll come up with something.

This is my first confession so I'm not sure exactly how well I did, but I did my best.

Your loving K.

(And yes the K is for killer, not very original I know, but there it is.)

58

"No wonder you couldn't come up with a motive," Anna is saying. "There isn't one."

We're on the phone later that afternoon as I stand out on our back patio looking at the lake and grilling steaks while there's still light enough to see what I'm doing.

Julia is serene, her mood unaffected, her beauty untouched by the storm from a few days ago.

Beyond her the setting sun leaves only a plum-colored smudge above the earth's western rim.

The burial shroud of night is once again being spread over the corpse of the Panhandle.

"Can you imagine being so nonchalant about killing a good man?" Anna says. "So unaffected by his murder— the murder you committed? The confession is a gaze into the dark abyss of an extremely demented soul—or absence of one."

"A true sociopath," I say.

"One that will most likely go unpunished," she says. "How do you catch a killer with no connection to the victim and no motive for their murder?"

"I wish I knew," I say.

The storm has interrupted and disrupted everything, including the investigation, but I refuse to let go of it or let the killer get away with it. Like life itself right now, it may be messy and difficult and broken, but I've got to keep putting one foot in front of the other.

"I've never read *Crime and Punishment*," she says. "I know it's Russian—Tolstoy or Dostoevsky, right? But what's the connection?"

"Yeah. Dostoevsky. Considered one of greatest novels ever written. A Russian law school dropout who lives in abject poverty kills his pawnbroker for her money, but after doing it is, unlike Andrew's killer, racked with guilt and remorse. It's a contemplation on morality, on human depravity, dignity, and grace."

"You think it inspired Andrew's murder?"

"No more than *The Catcher in the Rye* did John Lennon's. It's bullshit justification—an attempt to give the vile act a certain panache or cachet that it doesn't and cannot have."

"God, we're so fragile," she says. "A little antifreeze in some orange juice and . . ."

I think about how vulnerable and fragile the storm revealed us to be.

Dave covering Sting's song "Fragile" floats through my mind.

"I miss you so much," she says. "I want to come home right now. Can't stand being away from you, but especially right now. After what we've all been through, especially the girls . . . I just want us all together."

"I miss you more than I can say, but I'm glad you're out of this for now, that you all are."

"Well, if it weren't for the girls, I'd be right there with you," she says, "and even then . . . I'm not sure how long I can stay away. They miss you really bad too. They need to be close to their dad right now."

"Why don't y'all come back as soon as water and power are restored?" I say.

"We'll see. That may be too long."

When we've said our goodbyes, I walk around to the side of the house to put the steak packaging into the trash can.

At the corner of the house my movements trigger the solar motion sensor security light and I startle and reach for my weapon as I see a strange man standing there.

Then I realize it's the clothes I've washed by hand and

hung on a makeshift clothesline. It's not the first time I've done it. The strange man is me, is my clothes. What does it mean that I keep jumping when I encounter him?

59

Later that night after Merrill, Dad, and I ate steak with no sides after waiting awhile for Reggie and Brad, who never showed, I review all my notes from the case, going back over what Dawn and Levi and Tad and Maddy and Marie Ann Trainer and Jan and Melissa and Auburn and Peggy Munn told me. And what they didn't. I listen to the 911 call several times and read and reread the confession letter—all in the faint illumination of a flashlight alone in a dark house, quiet except for the sounds of generators in my neighborhood and linemen crews uptown coming through the screen of my open windows.

My generator is off. Given that it's just me and there's a shortage of gas and so many people don't have them—

even families with small children—I'd feel too guilty running it.

So I sit in the near dark of a humid and hot house with sweat trickling down my body.

Now that I know the killer's motive—or lack thereof—I am looking at and listening to everything again from a different perspective. Since motive and victimology aren't going to be much use, I've got to look at means, opportunity, and other elements to try to make the case. Of course, the confession could all be a lie meant to mislead or perhaps not even written by the killer, but I truly believe that it is the genuine article written by the person who on a whim robbed Andrew of his life.

911, what's your emergency?

Somebody's dead.

Who? What is the address?

The ex-priest in Wewa . . . He's dead. Been killed.

What's your address? Are you with him?

702

(Background) can . . . use forklift.

702 what?

No. Not—that was wrong. 788 North Highway 71.

(Background) We have a customer (inaudible) for treated two-by-fours.

Who am I speaking with?

You want his name?

What is your name?

Andrew Irwin.

Are you with the victim now, Andrew?

I'm not Andrew. He is.

The victim's name is Andrew? Can you wait with him until emergency services arrive?

No.

(Background) Loud truck engine. Maybe a child squealing. Maybe a dog barking in the distance. A horn beeping. A loud wooden crack like a bat hitting something maybe. Two men laughing loudly.

What is your name? Where are you?

(Inaudible)

(Background) Where you at? Need . . . help . . . sending him out. Hey big fella.

Hey, please don't do that. Please leave her alone, okay?

Please leave who alone? Are you okay? What is your name? Where are you? Sounds like a lot is going on there?

I'm not going to tell you any of that. Andrew is dead. Goodbye.

LISTENING to the 911 call this time, over and over like I'm doing, I begin to allow for the fact that the caller may not be a man at all, but a woman or a boy holding something over the phone to muffle the sound and lowering and disguising their voice. It could still be a man, but it could just as possibly not be.

My Confession

I killed Andrew Irwin. Or Father Andrew if you prefer. Makes no never mind to me. It's funny, I don't feel any guilt or remorse and yet the act of writing this down, of stating that I'm the one who did it so directly is creating a sensation in me I find hard to describe. I definitely feel lighter somehow. Not unburdened exactly, because . . .

I wanted to find someone with little or no connection to me but who was on their own so I wouldn't accidentally kill someone else or more than one person. So I began looking around and I came upon Andrew. He lives alone. He has no connection to me. And while it occurred to me that he was old and sort of sad and lonely, that really didn't factor in, but I did realize that he had already lived most of his life and that he wasn't having much of a life anyway.

If you had little or no connection to Andrew, how did you gain access to his house? His kitchen? His refrigerator?

How does a stranger do what Andrew's killer did? Break in? Enter under a different pretext? Or maybe not enter at all but have someone, perhaps even unwittingly, do it for you.

Of course, that part of the confession could be a lie. Maybe the killer isn't nearly as unconnected as the letter claims.

I go over everything again and again—over and over until I can no longer hold my head up or my eyes open.

When I wake up miserable, hot, and sweaty a few hours later, I think I know who killed Andrew.

I stumble to the bathroom, kneel down on the floor, and plunge my head into the cold water in the tub, then after toweling off, I return to my room to retrieve my phone to call Reggie.

60

"Did I wake you?" I ask.

"Fuck no," she says. "I've slept two hours in two days."

"You got a minute for me to run something past you?"

"You know who did it, don't you, you brilliant bastard?"

"It's thin," I say. "Very, very thin."

"What else could it be, given what he said in that confession letter?" she says. "Let's hear it."

"Joan Prescott," I say.

"The dog groomer girl?"

"Mary's hair and slobber were on Andrew when we found him," I say. "I think she was there when he died. Which means Joan didn't pick her up the night before but that morning. A dog barks in the background of the 911 call. I think it's Mary. I think Joan pulled into Ace to make the call from the warehouse phone and the dog can be heard from her convertible bug. I think Mary barked at an Ace worker or another customer getting lumber loaded into their truck. Someone says, 'Hey big fella.' Then Joan covers the phone and says, 'Hey, please don't do that. Please leave her alone, okay?' I remember looking at the calendar in Andrew's kitchen with all Mary's appointments on it—she had just been groomed. It wasn't time for her to go again. And there was a brand new bag of gourmet dog food in the corner by her bowl. I think Joan brought it from Bride and Grooming for Andrew and snuck in the poisoned orange juice while she was in there. Next morning she returns, places the blue plastic cross in Andrew's mouth and picks up Mary. Stops by Ace and tosses the antifreeze bottle in the dumpster and calls 911."

"That cunning little psychopath," she says. "It fits. It's thin, you're right. But it fits. Whatta you want to do?"

"Interview her again in the morning," I say. "Slip in Miranda and record her. Do it at her house, on her turf, see if I can get her to confess. She's already shown she wants to. She said she didn't but no one writes a letter like that who isn't wanting to. Maybe I can get her to brag about how clever she is, how much smarter than us she is."

"It's worth a shot," she says. "Not like we can do much more than that in our current condition anyway. And God knows fuckers who do shit like this love to brag about it in one way or another. Good work, John. Good work. Now go get her."

After we end the call, I try to get some sleep, but am too keyed up and too hot and sweaty.

Though I feel guilty to do so, I trudge to the other end of the house, go outside, crank the generator, and run the heavy-duty extension cord to my bedroom and plug in the window unit and a fan with it, justifying it by saying I need to get some sleep so I can get a confession in the morning.

I still find it difficult to sleep, but every time I do, every time I doze off for even a few minutes, I dream I'm being served orange juice and though I know it had antifreeze in it I keep drinking it anyway.

Before my alarm goes off the next morning, my phone rings, waking me from a dream in which the water from the tap that I am drinking suddenly and inexplicably turns to poisoned orange juice.

"Sorry to wake you," Reggie says. "But . . . I really thought you were right last night. Like you I thought it was thin, but I thought it fit."

"And now you don't?"

"We just got a call from Joan's dad," she says. "She's dead. Died just like Andrew—no blue plastic cross in her mouth, but from what he's describing I think she was killed the exact same way. Jessica's on her way over there now. Go meet her and figure out who this fuckin' serial killer is."

61

J essica Young is already processing the scene when I arrive.

After Reggie called I took my time showering and getting ready, thinking through everything while I did, trying to figure out where I went wrong. I had been fairly certain it was her. How could I have been so far off?

Joan Prescott is lying dead in her bed, her eyes open, staring up at nothing, covers flung back, her nightshirt bunched up around her, one arm hanging off the bed, facing up as if about to receive a shot.

Jessica hovers over the body taking pictures.

"FDLE is sending a team," she says. "No idea how long it'll take them to get here. I'm just gonna take pictures and temps until they do. They're gonna process what's left of the van and the body in it too and haul it back with them."

The bedroom is modest, even sort of Spartan—two twin beds separated by a nightstand, a small desk with a laptop on it, a small dresser with a small TV on it, a bookshelf, and a closet with colorful clothes but not many of them. The room gives the overall feel of not having been changed since early adolescence.

"Wonder why two beds?" I say.

"She's an only child, right?" Jessica says. "Probably for sleepover company when she was younger. I don't know. Bedroom looks sort of immature for her age. That's all your department."

I nod.

"Reggie said you suspected her of being the killer?"

"Yeah," I say, hoping her dad, who's sitting with a deputy in the living room, didn't hear her.

"Can't get it right every time," she says.

"Does it appear to be the same as Andrew?" I ask.

She nods. "I'd say identical. Can't be positive—I could be wrong too—but I'm betting the autopsy and lab results will show she died of the same thing."

I glance over at the mug of what looks to have been hot tea on the nightstand. The mug is meant to look like a dog, with a head sticking out one side and the tail forming a handle on the other. The little paper tab still hangs from the small string going to the tea bag inside the cup.

Noticing me looking at it, Jessica says, "We'll have it tested. But unless it was suicide or someone else made her cup of tea for her, it's probably not where she got it from."

Any of those scenarios are possible, I think. She kills Andrew and then herself. Or whoever killed Andrew made the tea for her and killed her too—or put it in something entirely different. But if in something else how could the killer know her dad wouldn't drink it too? Unless her dad is the killer or there's something she drinks that her dad doesn't and the killer knows it.

I step over and study her bookshelf, searching for a copy of *Crime and Punishment*, but there isn't one. And though there are some philosophy texts and novels mixed in, most of her books are about animals.

Remembering the killer's confession had said *Crime and Punishment* had been an audiobook, I turn back to Jessica. "Have you seen her phone?"

"Yeah, already bagged it," she says, nodding to the cardboard evidence box.

With gloved hands I find the phone in the box. It's in a sealed and signed clear plastic evidence bag that I pull out.

"What're you—"

"I need to check something," I say.

"You can't," she says. "Hasn't been printed or processed yet."

"Doesn't this have facial recognition?" I say.

"Not sure it will work in the bag."

"No problem with me trying, is there?" I say. "As long as I leave it in the bag."

"Just be careful and handle it as little as possible— even in the bag."

I hold the phone up to Joan's face and even through the plastic bag it unlocks.

"Wow," she says. "It's good to know that works."

I swipe through her apps until I find one for audiobooks and open it. There among the recently listened to, along with a crime thriller and a romance, is *Crime and Punishment*.

62

"She was just the sweetest thing," Petey Prescott is saying. "Or used to be. To everyone. But especially to animals. Boy, she loved animals. And they loved her. All her babies are going to be as heartbroken as I am. They're all at the neighbors right now—three dogs, four counting the one from that priest who died, and two cats. No way y'all'd be able to do anything if they were here. They'd be . . ." He breaks down and begins to cry, wiping at his puffy red eyes with crinkled and shedding wadded-up tissue. "Still can't believe she's gone. It's like it's not real. It's not real, is it? It can't be."

"I'm very sorry," I say.

He continues to cry and I wait a beat before saying anything else.

Eventually, I say, "What did you mean *or used to be*?"

He shakes his head, frowns, and wipes his eyes. "Joan was always different. It's hard to explain, but . . . knowing she had a twin who died, having her mother take off on us the way she did . . . She was . . . She was just never happy—not that anyone but me would know it. She had this like public persona where she was the happiest, most bubbly person. It was like there were two of her. They were very different, the public and the private Joans. But . . . since her wreck . . . everything has gotten so extreme. I mean . . . really extreme. I've been trying to figure out the best way to get her help. She didn't think she needed it, but I'm telling you it was like somebody swapped places with my little girl at the hospital after her wreck."

"Was her head injured in the car accident?" I ask.

He nods slowly. "Pretty severely. And that's what I've been suspecting more and more of being the real issue. I've just started doing some reading, but a brain injury, 'specially to the frontal lobe, would explain a lot of it I think."

I nod and think how it could also explain her murdering Father Andrew.

"Please don't share this with anyone," he says. "I know you won't. I don't know why I felt the need to say that, but . . . it's hard to say these things about my precious little angel. You have girls. You know what I mean. Her mood swings were epic and she got violent—something she's never been before. And the hallucinations or fantasies or whatever they were . . . were so bizarre. I mean . . . she was forgetting so much—both short-term and long-term stuff, but the stuff she remembered or thought she did . . . was just outlandish. She actually said she was having memories of being abused as a child—sexually abused by a priest. We weren't Catholic. Never went to church of any kind really. And the strangest thing of all . . . the way she would tell them . . . it was like she was a little boy—like an altar boy or something."

"I'm so sorry you've been dealing with this," I say. "I know a serious brain injury can completely change someone's personality. And you're right. It's truly not them."

"It wasn't her," he says, shaking his head. "And when I knew for sure was when she got fired for abusing the animals. My Joan would never do that, not in a million years. Sally McBride, the owner of Bride and Grooming, felt terrible, but . . . She even called me to explain and did so in an apologetic way, like it was her fault or something, but I can tell you . . . the things she told me Joan did to some of those animals . . . It was like close to damn torture and that wasn't her, wasn't like her at all. It was about as opposite her as you could get."

It all fits, I think. *All makes a lot more sense.*

"Any idea what she died of?" he asks. "Is it suspicious

in some way, that why y'all are here? I just can't help but think that it's got to be a result of the wreck. Like a delayed reaction or something. Which is probably why she's been getting worse lately."

"We won't know for sure until the autopsy and lab work are done," I say. "But someone this young and no obvious cause of death . . . We're going to take good care of her and find out exactly what happened. And it could be related to her car accident, even indirectly."

He nods. "I appreciate that. I want to know. I just can't imagine what it could be . . . unless . . .

"Unless?"

"Unless . . . she was born with some issue or defect we didn't know about," he says. "I told you she was a twin. Well, her sister was born dead. It's why she always insisted on those twin beds. Had to have a bed for Jill. Anyway if it wasn't the car accident . . . I wonder if whatever Jill died of . . . is what finally got Joan too."

"We'll find out and let you know," I say. "Anything different about last night or the past few days for her?"

He shakes his head.

"Nothing out of the ordinary?" I ask "No visitors? No workers in or around the house because of the storm or anything?"

He shakes his head. "No. Nothing like that. I mean, nothing is normal because of the storm. Joan was here,

stuck at home, no job to go to, nothing to do, but . . .
nothing unusual. I guess. Truth is . . . I wasn't around a
lot. I've been helping with the cleanup. I've got a truck
and trailer and a couple of chainsaws. Been trying to help
clear driveways so people can at least get in and out of
their homes. Helped blue roof a few homes too. Come
home hot and exhausted and it's dark and there's nothing
to do so I'd crash. Last . . . Last few nights of her life . . . we
hardly saw each other."

He breaks down again.

Jessica appears in the hallway and motions me back
to Joan's room.

"Just take your time," I say to Petey. "Excuse me for
one minute. I'll be right back. And again, I'm so sorry."

By the time I reach the end of the hallway, Jessica is
back inside Joan's room.

She's holding a jewelry box with gloved hands, and
when I walk into the room she reaches in and pulls out
the felt covered organizer to reveal a false bottom and the
contents beneath.

I tap on the flashlight on my phone and shine it
inside.

There, hidden in the recesses of the secret compart-
ment, is a rosary like the one Father Andrew owned, an
old man's little black comb, and a lock of gray hair.

"Found this too," she says, pulling a journal out from

beneath the jewelry box. "I only glanced at it, but the little I saw was some dark and disturbing shit."

I nod. "Good work, Jessica. Thank you."

"I think you were right after all," she says. "But if that's true . . . If she killed Andrew . . . who killed her?"

63

"You figured it out before I did," I say. "And you killed her."

"So she's dead then?" Peggy Munn says.

I find her sitting on the front pew in the darkened sanctuary of St. Lawrence, not far from where her beloved Andrew had been found.

I had been on my way to check on Auburn McLemore to make sure my ill-advised reaction to Levi yesterday hadn't resulted in another beating for her, when I realized who had killed Joan—who it had to be.

"Couldn't let it stand," she says. "Couldn't let that wicked girl kill my Andrew like that and not do anything about it. So I gave her a dose of her own medicine."

I nod.

The sanctuary is warm, humid, and beginning to

smell of mold and mildew and I wonder what will become of it. Beyond its walls the heavy traffic on the highway can be heard—trucks and trailers hauling in workers and supplies, hauling out trash and debris.

"A decent and kind man who spent his life helping others and she just . . . just poisoned him like some rat or something. Why? Why did she do it?"

"Because her mind was sick. Because she had a brain injury."

"But why? What did she have against him? What was the real reason she—"

"Nothing," I say. "She had nothing against him. He had done nothing to her. She just . . . she just wanted to kill someone and she picked him."

"I don't understand," she says.

"You'd have to be a sociopath in order to," I say.

"But . . . How . . . Oh, my Lord. What a twisted, evil little girl."

"You killed her out of revenge," I say. "Out of a certain sense of retribution because of your love for Andrew and your hatred of the person who took him from you. Most people can understand that. That's a motive most of us can relate to in some way, but to just pick a person, decide it's their day to die . . . It's unfathomable to most of us."

"She just picked him," she says, "and . . . poisoned him . . . for no real reason at all. I just don't get it."

I pull out my phone and pull up some of the pictures I took of Joan's journal.

"She was unstable to begin with," I say, "but she was in a bad car wreck and sustained a head trauma. She has been deteriorating for a while now. This is from her diary: 'Everything is fucked. It's not just me. It's the whole world. Sure, there can be a pretty day—the sun shining and everything seems pleasant, but that's just like the smile I paste on my face and the perky little hippy chick animal lover act I put on. It's a facade. Not real. I really think I should have died with Jill, that I'm not really meant to be here. I should have been born dead and then I should have died in the car crash. Is that why God lets me suffer so much? Because I'm supposed to be dead? Why else would he let me lose my sister and my mom and then let me be abused by the man who claims to represent him? I was little and helpless and just there to serve. Maybe I am dead already. I could be and not know it. This could be what hell is like. I'm certainly tormented. Well, if I'm dead, he should be too. What would it be like to kill someone? To feel the power of God-fucking-almighty in your fingertips. If I kill someone—anyone—will God kill me? Eye for an eye. Tooth for a tooth. Random death for a random death. Maybe I can't be killed. I mean, seems like he's been trying a while. What if . . . What if I'm God? Wouldn't that be a trip? I'm not God. There is no God. There's just chaos. Just suffering behind our stupid faces with the insipid smiles plastered on them. I don't know. I don't even know what I'm saying. I'm just so tired. So ready for my head to stop hurting. Going to sleep now. Maybe I'll wake up and kill someone tomorrow.'"

"My Lord," Peggy says.

"There's an entire journal full of that," I say.

"I put a very sick child out of her misery," she says. "But if I had known she was that . . . ill . . . I might not have. Or maybe . . . as she said . . . she killed someone and God killed her."

"Neither one of you were doing the work of God," I say.

"I know," she says. "I was just . . . I wasn't being literal. I don't mind going to prison. I have no life without Andrew. And don't want one. Not that this old body has much life left in it anyway."

"You might have more than you think," I say. "And you might change your mind. And if ever an act of murder had mitigating circumstances . . . You're obviously not a danger to society. And there's not a jury member in the world that wouldn't sympathize with you, wouldn't relate to why you did what you did. So hire a good attorney and defend yourself and explain yourself and take the opportunity to share Andrew with others as you do."

"I . . . I guess I could do that," she says. "I don't know though. I'm awfully tired. And I miss him so much."

"The more time you have outside of prison, the more time you'd have to take care of Mary," I say. "That'd give you a part of Andrew to—"

"That's the excuse I used to get into her house," she says. "Told her I wanted to talk to her about Mary, about her coming to live with me. She didn't want to give her up. I went back and forth with her and acted like a doddering old lady, used her rest room a few times, moved slowly in everything I did, and lingered and lingered until she finally went outside to make a phone call and I slipped the antifreeze in the soda she was drinking. Didn't want to put it in something that Petey might drink. But . . . I really would love to have Mary, to care for her the way he did—for him. I'd really like that."

"I'm sure he would too," I say.

"Do you think Anna would represent me?"

"I'm not sure she can since I'm the arresting officer."

"Are you here to arrest me?" she asks.

"I'm afraid I am," I say. "I don't like it much, but . . . that is what I'm here to do."

64

A s it turns out I wasn't there to arrest her. Since we have no functional jail and courthouse at the moment and since she poses neither a flight risk nor a danger to the community, Reggie says just to put the case and the arrest on pause for now.

"We have much bigger issues to deal with than a little old lady who did our job for us," Reggie had said.

So Peggy is home with her new houseguest Mary.

And our post-storm life, the new not-normal normal continues.

Trucks continue rolling loudly up and down the road. Chainsaws and generators continue to be the soundtrack. People continue to sit on their porches as if we're suddenly back in a bygone era. Meals mostly consist of meat grilled outside or MREs—add water and take the recommended laxative. Supplies continue to pour into the old gym and continue to be passed out by upbeat teenagers who gladly give a cup of water and a whole lot more in His name. Hanging clothes continue to appear to be menacing strangers. Water continues to come on just a few hours a day. Cell service continues to be only in certain spots and only spotty even in them. Bodies continue to be discovered in the debris. Rumors continue to make the rounds. The amped-up police presence and the curfew continue. The kindness of strangers continues.

And the post-storm death toll continues to rise.

A lineman from North Carolina is killed because of how a homeowner illegally jury-rigged his generator, which sent 220 volts of current out to the street and the main line he was working on.

But by far the most personally devastating call is the one that comes one week and one day since Michael roared in and wreaked havoc.

Brad Price is killed when a tree falls on him and the tractor he is using to clear debris.

I am stunned.

And I find his arbitrary and accidental death as random and capricious as that of Father Andrew's—two very different forces behind them, but each just as tragic and inexplicable and unexpected as the other.

And then the town stops.

For the first time since the storm was on top of us, everyone stops.

And we make our way to Main Street in the dark night, only a smudge of cloud-covered moon above us.

Lining up along the sidewalk as if for one of our many small-town parades, we comfort one another with hugs and handshakes and exchange stories about Brad and the way he had touched our lives in so very many ways.

As I stand there with my neighbors, I'm grateful again to be in this tiny town that produces people like Brad.

Overhead in the dark night sky a helicopter flies by, bringing Brad's daughter back from Panama City Beach so she can participate in the processional about to take place.

Mixed in among the citizens are firefighters and highway patrol officers and other emergency services workers, each waiting like us to honor their fallen colleague, the lights of their vehicles flashing behind them.

Some of them have hung a huge American flag on the massive limb of an oak tree that stretches across Main Street near the Methodist church and lit it from beneath with a bank of halogen work lamps.

And then the whine of the siren starts.

Escorted by law enforcement and emergency services vehicles and firetrucks, all with their lights flashing, the ambulance carrying Brad's body is led from his house, through town, down Main Street, beneath the waving American flag in between sidewalks lined with mourners and other firefighters saluting.

Looking on in reverential and stunned silence, fresh tears trickle down the faces of shocked friends and family and grateful citizens who thought they had seen the last of death and destruction and shed the last of their tears for a while.

At the intersection of Main Street and Highway 22 where the processional turns to head to Panama City, a line of firemen stand at an angle across the road and salute as the vehicle bearing the body of the fallen hero passes by.

When the wail of the siren fades in the distance and the only sounds left are the generator powering the lone stoplight in town and the sniffles of those mournfully lining the street, slowly people begin to peel off and disappear back into the darkness.

A few minutes after I arrive home, the electricity in town comes back on, and we are told that we are running on an enormous generator on loan from Texas and that it will still be several weeks or longer before the transmission lines that can actually carry current to us will be rebuilt and restored.

Regardless, having our electricity on is a small step in the long journey of our recovery, and though it inspires some small seed of hope it is also odd and disconcerting,

coming as it does on the backdrop of the somber processional we've just returned home from.

I call Anna to let her know our power has been
restored and to see if I can talk her into coming back
home tomorrow, but when she answers there is something unusual in her voice.

"Is everything okay?" I ask.

"It's about to be."

"I was calling to let you know that the electricity in
town just came back on."

"Perfect timing," she says. "Turn on the outside lights
and come help me unload."

"You're—"

"In the driveway," she says. "With some little girls that
miss their daddy—but not as much as their mama misses
their daddy. Started loading up the moment you called
about Brad. Couldn't be away from you another
moment."

65

In our bed together, freshly showered and in the coolness of an air-conditioned room, Anna and I hold each other in the dark.

Tomorrow I will face the post-apocalyptic world again, and I will continue to try to find the men from the hurricane house and the stolen van, but for now, there is only now, only this, only Anna.

"I don't think I've ever taken this for granted," she whispers, "but I certainly know I don't now. And won't for the foreseeable future."

"As grateful as I've always been for you, for getting to be with you," I say, "it feels even more intense now."

"I feel so broken up for Brad's loved ones," she says. "How much more can that storm take from us?"

"I really wish you hadn't asked that," I say.

"Was a stupid thing to verbalize," she says. "But I've certainly been wondering it."

"Yeah, I think we all have."

"Next time I start to say something stupid like that, you should cover my lips with yours," she says, and kisses me.

After kissing for a few moments we are quiet and I may have dozed off.

"Huh?" I say.

"Poor thing," she says. "Go to sleep."

"No. Not yet. What did you say?"

"Just that I feel bad for Peggy. I can't help it. I feel bad for what she lost and for what she felt she had to do about it."

"If I had been a little quicker I could've saved her from doing what she did."

"Interesting choice of words," she says. "*Saved.*"

"I just meant—"

"No, I know. But I find your savior complex sexy. I really do. You saved our girls. And our boy in a round-about way. Just don't want you always feeling like you have to save the world."

"I don't," I say. "I absolutely do not. Not in any way."

"Me thinks he doth protest too much," she says.

"Maybe you should put your lips over mine to shut me up," I say.

"That's a great idea," she says. "Whoever came up with that is a genius."

She begins kissing me, and murders and superstorms and saving anyone all fade into nothing and there is only us, our lips, our kisses, our bodies, our love, our connection in this moment.

And in spite of everything, I am hopeful.

Our journey toward recovery has just begun, but it has begun.

And I'm in bed with my dream girl, and our girls are safe and secure in a room of their own not far away.

I'm not sure how long Anna and I make love again, not sure how long we've been asleep when my phone starts ringing on the bedside table, but when I open my eyes I can see that it is light outside.

"No rest for the weary," Reggie says. "One of the bodies found in the rubble of one of the homes at the beach looks like it may have been dead before it was put there, long before the storm roared ashore."

"On my way," I say, and ease out of bed to once again enter the fray of a world I'm convinced is worth fighting for.

EPILOGUE

Hurricane Michael began in the southwest Caribbean Sea and was first monitored by the National Hurricane Center on October 2, 2018. By October 8, 2018 it strengthened into a hurricane, and by the time it made landfall at Mexico Beach, Florida, on October 10th, it was a Category 4 storm—the first such to hit the Florida Panhandle in recorded history. And many experts believe that it will eventually be upgraded to a Category 5. The property damage is estimated at over $4.5 billion and continuing to climb. Hurricane Michael, with 155 mph sustained winds and 200 mph gusts at landfall, is in the top 3 strongest storms to ever make landfall in the continental United States. A fast moving and fast developing superstorm that didn't give residents time to prepare or evacuate, Hurricane Michael rapidly intensified by 45 mph just in the last 24 hours leading up to landfall. Of the nearly 8 billion people on the planet, very few have or will ever experience anything like Hurricane Michael.

ALSO BY MICHAEL LISTER

Books by Michael Lister

(John Jordan Novels)

Power in the Blood

Blood of the Lamb

Flesh and Blood

(Special Introduction by Margaret Coel)

The Body and the Blood

Double Exposure

Blood Sacrifice

Rivers to Blood

Burnt Offerings

Innocent Blood

(Special Introduction by Michael Connelly)

Separation Anxiety

Blood Money Blood Moon

Thunder Beach

Blood Cries

A Certain Retribution

Blood Oath

Blood Work

Cold Blood

Blood Betrayal

Blood Shot

Blood Ties

Blood Stone

Blood Trail

Bloodshed

Blue Blood

And the Sea Became Blood

(Jimmy Riley Novels)

The Girl Who Said Goodbye

The Girl in the Grave

The Girl at the End of the Long Dark Night

The Girl Who Cried Blood Tears

The Girl Who Blew Up the World

(Merrick McKnight / Reggie Summers Novels)

Thunder Beach

A Certain Retribution

Blood Oath

Blood Shot

(Remington James Novels)

Double Exposure

(includes intro by Michael Connelly)

Separation Anxiety

Blood Shot

(Sam Michaels / Daniel Davis Novels)

Burnt Offerings

Blood Oath

Cold Blood

Blood Shot

(Love Stories)

Carrie's Gift

(Short Story Collections)

North Florida Noir

Florida Heat Wave

Delta Blues

Another Quiet Night in Desperation

(The Meaning Series)

<u>Meaning Every Moment</u>

<u>The Meaning of Life in Movies</u>